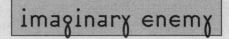
imaginary enemy

Also by Julie Gonzalez

Ricochet

Wings

imaginary enemy
JULIE GONZALEZ

LAUREL-LEAF BOOKS

Published by Laurel-Leaf
an imprint of Random House Children's Books
a division of Random House, Inc.
New York

Originally published in hardcover in the United States by Delacorte Press, New York, in 2008. This edition published by arrangement with Delacorte Press.

Laurel-Leaf and colophon are registered trademarks of Random House, Inc.

Visit us on the Web! www.randomhouse.com/teens

Educators and librarians, for a variety of teaching tools, visit us at
www.randomhouse.com/teachers

The Library of Congress has cataloged the hardcover edition of this work as follows:
Gonzalez, Julie.
Imaginary enemy / Julie Gonzalez.
  p. cm.
Summary: Although her impetuous behavior, smart-mouthed comments, and slacker ways have landed her in trouble over the years, sixteen-year-old Jane has always put the blame on her "imaginary enemy," until a new development forces her to decide whether or not to assume responsibility for her actions.
ISBN: 978-0-385-73552-0 (trade) — ISBN: 978-0-385-90530-5 (Gibraltar lib. bdg.)
[1. Behavior—Fiction. 2. Responsibility—Fiction.] I. Title.
PZ7.G5931m 2008
[Fic]—dc22
2007045752

ISBN: 978-0-440-24070-9 (pbk.)
Reprinted by arrangement with Delacorte Press
RL: 5.5
July 2009
Printed in the United States of America
10 9 8 7 6 5 4 3 2 1

First Laurel-Leaf Edition

To Cecile and Herning

Kate and "that rabbit"

And imaginary friends and enemies everywhere

You never liked to get
The letters that I sent.
But now you've got the gist
Of what my letters meant.

LEONARD COHEN
AND SHARON ROBINSON

Spilled Milk

I t's not unusual to have an imaginary friend. Many people do (or did, at any rate, somewhere in their histories). But me? I can honestly tell you that I have no imaginary friend. Not one.

What I have is an imaginary enemy. He's such a satisfying companion—very therapeutic to have around. He's helped me through a number of personal disasters and misadventures over the years. I call my imaginary enemy Bubba—short for Beelzebub, which is a biblical devil's name. Pretty good way to address an enemy, wouldn't you agree?

Bubba's not necessarily physically unattractive, but this is one of those "it's what's on the inside that counts" situations. 'Cause that's where Bubba reveals his true colors—on the inside. He's a sneak and a liar and a troublemaker who delights in seeing my life go wrong. My miseries are his homemade ice cream. My heartbreaks are his Godiva chocolates. My failures are his double cheeseburgers and deep-dish pizzas. You get the picture.

When Bubba makes me angry, I write him a letter expressing my displeasure. The first time I wrote to Bubba was in second grade.

> Dear Budda,
>   You spilled milk on the lunchroom floor. I slipped in it and ripped a hole in my new overalls. My knee bled. Everyone laughed. I don't like you.
>   Sinfully yours,
>   Gabriel

Gabriel isn't my real name. It's just the name I use in my relationship with Bubba. No point in being overly familiar with an enemy, especially an imaginary one. Gabriel, like Bubba, is biblical—one of the heavenly superstars, along with his pals Michael and Raphael. Gabriel is chief of the archangels—God's right-hand halo polisher. Kind of like vice president if God is top dog. I imagine him to have beautiful ivory-colored wings tipped with moonlight and a halo of red gold that undulates like the ripples on the surface of a pond.

With my Bubba letter clasped in my hand, I asked my teacher, Mrs. Perkins, for a piece of tape, but when she realized I wanted to hang my message on the classroom wall, she refused. "Jane, why are you writing Buddha a letter about spilled milk?" she asked.

"Buddha?"

"The founder of the religion Buddhism. He was a very wise spiritual leader."

"Not Buddha, *Bubba*," I replied insistently. Cold air

from the air conditioner breezed though the hole in the knee of my overalls.

Mrs. Perkins raised her eyebrow. Just one eyebrow. That was the coolest thing about her—she could raise her left eyebrow like a marine raising the flag up the pole. "Then you inverted your lowercase Bs again." She tapped the letter. "Who's Bubba?"

"A dirty rotten milk-spilling creep," I answered.

"Go sit down and behave yourself, Jane." Mrs. Perkins sounded exasperated. I stalked back to my seat clutching Bubba's letter and stashed it in my math folder. A fairly modest beginning to what has proven to be a long and fruitless relationship.

Since you know my name's not really Gabriel, I might as well tell you the three embarrassing appellations my parents attached to my birth certificate sixteen years ago. I can't believe they did me such dishonor. Start with Jane. That's *J-A-N-E*. As in Plain Jane, which the more poetic schoolyard bullies have called me since kindergarten. Along with Birdbrain Jane, Migraine Jane, and Jane the Pain. All because my parents named me after this prehistoric aunt of Mom's who they particularly admire.

My middle name's even worse. Venezuela—like the South American country. Great name for a country. Very lyrical and seductive. But a middle name for a girl? Venezuela? That's where my parents met. It was nothing terribly romantic if you ask me. My mother was visiting her college roommate, a beautiful but unsuccessful South American poet, and my recently divorced father was on a fishing vacation with his brother, my uncle Grayson. Dad's cooler of semifrozen baitfish leaked on Mom's suitcase in the hotel elevator, and she insisted he buy her a new one because of the awful smell and the stains. Who knew they'd end up with a bunch of kids and a dog? When I complain about my name, Dad thinks it's a real laugh to say, "We could have named you Caracas instead of Jane." (For the geographically impaired, Caracas is the capital of Venezuela.)

Now (drumroll, please) for my absolutely generic last name: White. Like clouds or snow or cotton. Like flour or sugar or milk. Like boredom.

When I was just over a year old, my parents got frisky. My brother Lysander was born nine and a half months later. He's named after one of the confused, love-struck youths in Shakespeare's *A Midsummer Night's Dream* (Dad's a Shakespeare freak). My brother hates his name. Go figure. He tells everyone to call him Zander.

Sixteen months after Zander came my sister, Carmella, whose name evokes visions of bonfires, gypsy music, starlit nights, and silver bangles. Me Jane, Plain Jane—You Carmella. Talk about a prize-winning recipe for some vicious sibling rivalry.

> *Dear Bubba,*
>
> *Shakespeare might have his "What's in a name?" thing, but he wasn't dubbed Jane Venezuela White. Why would you ever allow anyone to go through life being addressed so blandly? And you claim to love me.*
>
> *A rose by any other name,*
> *Gabriel*

My half brother, Luke, who's five years older than me, sat by my side on the sofa playing a video game. He's the offspring of Dad's youthful marriage to his high-school sweetheart, Sandy. "Gotcha," Luke said as his character zapped mine. The screen lit up in neon blue flashes as my player sizzled and lost a dose of power.

"Bully," I snarled.

He laughed. "No crybabies allowed."

"I'm no crybaby," I protested. *Crybaby* was the ultimate insult someone could hurl at an ornery seven-year-old.

"Pay attention, loser!" He detonated his weapon and my character strobed once again.

I pushed a pulsating radioactive boulder over him. "Take that!"

His character fizzled out in a puff of purple smoke. "Yikes!" he exclaimed, laughing.

"I like it when you come over," I said. Luke spent Wednesdays and alternate weekends with us. And sometimes he came for unscheduled visits. This was one of those. He'd ridden his bike to our house after school.

"I like it here. And you have a dog. Mom won't let me have a pet," Luke said, tossing the game controller aside and dragging his fingers through Banjo's fur.

"Maybe she's allergic. Like Peggy next door. Dogs make her sneeze and itch."

"Naw. Mom says we're not home enough for a dog. That they need lots of attention. And Marty thinks they're a mess. All that fur and stuff bugs him." Marty is Luke's stepfather.

"Well, Banjo's your dog, too," I said, feeling a generosity of spirit at the time.

"Marty sucks."

"Dad says he's okay."

"What does he know?"

"Why don't you like him?"

Luke shrugged. Something about his demeanor made me feel like I was the older sibling. "I just don't."

"Is he mean?"

Luke shrugged again. Banjo, so named because as a pup he was described by our neighbor Elliot as being "wound tighter than a banjo string," climbed into Luke's lap and nuzzled his neck. "He's just . . . I don't know . . . he's always telling me what to do. And how to do it. And what not to do. And how not to do it. It's not like he's my real dad."

"My mom tells you what to do when you're here."

"Yeah, sometimes. But not in the same way. She treats me like she treats you and Zander and Carmella. Marty—he never makes his little princess do anything."

"You mean Lainey?"

"Who else? And why should I get stuck babysitting *his* kid? I hate it when she's there." Lainey, Luke's stepsister, is around my age. I'd played with her a few times. Just a week earlier, she'd been with Sandy when she brought Luke over for the weekend. All the adults were talking, so Lainey and I ran around the yard collecting leaves.

"I think Lainey's nice," I told Luke.

"She's boring. And spoiled. All she has to do is whine and she gets whatever she wants. I can't believe my mother lets her get away with that stuff. . . . It sure never worked for me."

"Maybe you're a brat, too, and just don't know it."
"Funny, Jane. Too funny."

It's always weird to imagine my father married to someone other than my mother—to picture pleasant little family scenes like we have but with a different supporting cast. Not Luke so much, because he's been around my whole life. But Sandy . . . Did my father really have a life before us? Did they go on picnics and gather around Christmas trees? Did he come up behind Sandy and wrap his arms around her waist when she stood at the sink washing dishes? Take her to those family functions at Grandma's that Mom attends now? In some irrational way, it seems traitorous to me.

The yard next door to ours has always been the most tangled musical paradise on earth. The lawn, which is exceptionally large, slopes gently away from the house. The grass is thick and lush and nearly always overgrown, which used to make it a spongy cushion for our wild childhood games. I loved the way it felt when it brushed my bare legs with feathery tickles. I liked the wild rabbits, snakes, beetles, and katydids that hid in its green carpet. Studding the yard are several ancient live oaks wrapped in vines that weave their tendrils into the bark and dangle from the heights like serpents in a snake-a-phobe's worst nightmare. But all that's only part of what sets the deMicheal property apart from everyone else's.

Our neighbor Elliot deMichael is a musician. He and his family moved in next door before I could walk. Back then, Elliot was working on his PhD. His thesis had something to do with major and minor scales in nature. That was what inspired him to turn his yard into a musical theme park. The trees are festooned with a smorgasbord of wind chimes he made from things like sticks and stones and alligator bones. He recorded the songs the wind wrote there and somehow worked them into his dissertation.

Palm trees line the back fence. "I don't care so much for the way they look," he once admitted, "but there is nothing to compare with the concerto of the rain and wind in their fronds."

Elliot built fountains and waterfalls whose music he records and charts. I used to sit at the patio picnic table with his kids and watch as he rearranged the stone tiers of some water garden to get a new progression of sound. He's wired bird feeders to steal the secret conversations of hungry but unsuspecting blue jays and finches. He has even bugged a wasps' nest with a miniature microphone. He's like the CIA of the natural world.

Elliot checks the weather report daily. If a storm or strong winds are predicted, he'll drag fancy equipment from the garage and set it up outside, covering it with tarps or plastic bags, and snake waterproof microphones to locations all over the yard to catch Mother Nature singing in the shower. He records thunder and rain and wind. Twilight with its dance of insects. Crickets fiddling the night away. Frogs croaking in deep bass tones.

To earn a living, Elliot teaches at the university and has a studio at home where he gives private lessons to aspiring musicians. When his students are there, his children are banished to the backyard, where my siblings and I often join them.

Considering Elliot deMichael's obsession, it's no surprise that all four of his children have musical names—Chord, Sharp, Jazz, and Harmony. His wife, Peggy, a lawyer, didn't mind indulging her husband's whims, and always teases their children, saying, "Besides, who'd want kids named Habeas Corpus, Sidebar, or Deposition?"

Chord is a year and a half older than Sharp and me and has always been a grade ahead of us in school, a fact he used to flaunt as proof of his superiority. As for Sharp, he and I were best friends until about middle school, when we went our separate ways, mine being predictably mainstream, his being increasingly unconventional.

Sharp and Chord both have blue-green eyes and unruly light brown hair as overgrown as the grass in their backyard, and as randomly curly as the tendrils springing from the vines in the live oaks. That's why they're often mistaken for twins. It happened all the time when they were younger. The resemblance is purely physical, though. In personality they're opposites, Chord being outspoken and abrupt, and Sharp quiet and easygoing.

One Saturday morning, Elliot invited Zander, Carmella, and me into his studio (his children were already there), promising us heavenly delights. My mouth watered in anticipation as I imagined ice cream sundaes and platters heaped with pastries. Elliot closed the blinds and clicked an icon on his PC. Recorded rain dripped from the speakers lining the room.

"Rain sounds different beneath the peach tree than it does when it splashes into the fountain," he said softly.

"And what a racket it makes on banana leaves," he added, clicking the mouse. "And the kiss of the dew on the grass—sublime!"

At that point I could barely hear anything, but Zander's eyes were shining. "Do it again!" he said.

"And now," Elliot announced, beaming with pride, "when I blend them all together . . . listen."

"Hey, that's Beethoven's Fifth!" exclaimed Sharp.

"In raindrops," said Chord. "Too cool."

"Beethoven's fifth what?" I asked innocently (or ignorantly, maybe).

"You're really stupid, you know?" said Chord, rolling his eyes. "Dumber than a box of rocks."

"What are you doing?" Zander asked. I jumped because I'd been unaware of his presence. He was standing in the doorway with Jazz, his best pal. I glared at both of their reflections in the bathroom mirror. Zander and Jazz, the same age, are practically inseparable. They act more like brothers than neighbors—fighting one minute and scheming together the next, taking one another's belongings without asking, and exploiting each other's flaws.

"Nothing." I stepped away from the mirror.

"Why are you making those nasty faces?" asked Jazz.

"I'm practicing, creep."

"Practicing what?"

"You know my teacher, Mrs. Perkins?"

"Yeah."

"Well, she does this eyebrow thing, and I'm trying to—"

"What eyebrow thing?" interrupted Zander.

"Like this," I said, and I used my hand to lift one eyebrow halfway up my forehead.

"Yuck. That's creepy." Even as Zander spoke, I noticed him and Jazz peering into the glass and contorting their faces.

"It's great when she does it. Wait till you get to second grade. If she's your teacher, you'll see." I tried again to do the trick, hands free.

"You look like you swallowed something gross," observed Zander.

"Go away."

They just stood there. Jazz pushed his left eyebrow, trying to make it do a Mrs. Perkins.

"I said go away, clones." I shoved them out the door and slammed it.

Turtle Power

My second letter to Bubba was inspired by a more serious set of circumstances than simple spilled milk. The incident occurred about three weeks after that soggy mishap. My father was reading an insurance company publication. He had an orange highlighter in his hand and every now and then he marked a passage. "These new depreciation charts could certainly be useful. I need to make a copy of this for Jim," he said, but no one was listening. I could think of few topics more boring, and I didn't even know what depreciation charts were.

Zander and I were playing checkers on the floor while Carmella watched cartoons. My mother walked into the room. "Kids, Peggy told me her boys got their report cards today. Where are yours?"

I ignored her, moving a checker to block Zander's potential double jump.

"In my backpack," my brother said. He scrambled down the hall to his room.

"Jane, I'd like to see your report card," said my father. I

studied the game board like it was the Rosetta Stone: the key to some universal secret.

Zander returned, digging through his backpack, and finally extracted a crumpled but stellar assessment of his academic and social progress. "What a good kindergartener you are!" Mom said proudly after looking it over. "Did you see what Ms. Golden wrote about you?"

"No," answered Zander.

"I'll read it. 'Zander is a pleasure to teach. He shows great potential.' "

"Oh," said Zander. "What's *po . . . po . . .* that word mean?"

"That you can achieve anything you attempt," Mom said.

"Great job, son," said Dad, slapping Zander's palm. "Jane, what about yours?"

I ignored him.

"Jane, your report card," he said louder.

"I think I left it at school," I muttered.

"Go look. Now," directed Mom. "It's probably in your backpack."

"But I'm playing checkers with Zander," I protested.

"Now, Jane."

Needless to say, my report card wasn't heavily embellished with As, or even Bs. And my delusional parents thought I was a closet genius. Whatever. I reluctantly went to my room and riffled through my school stuff until I unearthed the manila envelope that contained my passport to doom. I handed it to my father with the nervous delicacy one might use when passing off a live grenade. Dad slipped my report card from the envelope (an act remarkably similar to removing the pin from a grenade), scrutinized it carefully, then read the comments Mrs. Perkins had written on the back. Those were mostly about my behavior, and she had used a significant population of long, menacing words. (I admit to having consulted the dictionary when I'd braved a glance at it earlier.) I stood there holding my breath and crossing my fingers behind my back. Dad, looking displeased, laid his magazine on the coffee table.

"Jane, sit down," he said, handing the offending document to my mother. I perched myself on the edge of the sofa. Dad shifted in his chair so that he was boring into me with his eyes. "I'm awfully disappointed in you," he said in his "this is serious business" voice. "I know you can do much better than this. You're a smart little girl, you just don't apply yourself. And the bad behavior . . . there's no excuse for that."

I got the usual lecture laced with threats and predictions about my future, which looked bleak. ("Do you want to end up unemployable because you have no regard for the rules? Do you want to spend your life waiting tables at Waffle House?") The natural follow-up to a good verbal thrashing is "Go to your room," and I was relieved when Dad finally said exactly that and I was able to escape the onslaught of his words.

I kicked the checkerboard, sending checkers bouncing across the floor. Then I stomped down the hall, slammed the door, and shoved my backpack off my bed. The rest—well, the rest was karma. My blue math folder tumbled out and spilled open, and there I saw my original letter to Bubba. I was inspired.

I snatched my math worksheet (that night's homework, which I hadn't been planning to do anyhow) and a pencil (the NASCAR one I stole from Matthew Sellers, who sat next to me) and gave Bubba a piece of my mind. I was careful not to invert my Bs this time, not wanting my letter to inadvertently fall into the wrong hands—those being the hands of the wise and spiritual religious leader Buddha.

> Dear Bubba,
>   You totally suck. I can't believe you put my name on your sorry report card. You are such a loser.
>
>   Go to heaven,
>   Gabriel

Bubba hates to be told to go to heaven. The very idea scares the tar out of him. He thinks only sissies wear halos and white robes.

I grabbed my green crayon and wrote "Bubba" in big letters on the front of my math folder. Then I crammed that letter into the pocket.

Sharp executed an exaggerated kick and sang out, "Teenage Mutant Ninja Turtles," initiating one of our favorite backyard games, inspired by the deMichaels' vast collection of turtle DVDs. He tossed a handful of colorful strips of fabric onto the picnic table.

"Heroes on the half shell," crooned Jazz and Zander together, slashing their hands through the air.

"I'm Donatello," I called. "He's the brainy one."

"No. You're a girl. You have to be April O'Neil," said Chord.

I stamped my foot. "I'm not going to be April. She's boring. I'm going to be a turtle, and Donatello's my favorite."

"I'm Splinter," said Jazz, claiming the role of the rat, "so there's an extra turtle anyway. Let her be Donatello."

"Yeah," agreed Zander, "we need all four turtles."

"I'm Leonardo." Sharp was tying a strip of ragged blue fabric around his head.

"Raphael," called Zander.

"*You* be April, Chord," I said.

"No way. I'm Michelangelo," said Chord, jabbing and kicking in an aerial calligraphy. "Although Jane should be the goofy one and I should be the smart one, all things considered."

"You should be roadkill," I snarled as I fastened a purple band around my head.

"Good one, Jane," said Sharp, slapping me a high five.

Chord, in his role as Michelangelo, got a queasy look on his face. "I think I'm gonna hurl, dudes. I ate too much pizza before that last gnarly encounter with Shredder's gang."

"A wise man does not overindulge," commented Jazz in a fairly good imitation of Splinter, the turtles' mentor. He shook his head and squinted in an attempt to look rat-like. With his shaggy honey-colored hair and large brown eyes, he looked more like a frisky puppy.

"Master Splinter, there is news that Shredder and his gang are planning another assault on the city," said Zander.

"We will prepare," said Jazz wisely.

And so we spent the afternoon ninja fighting on and around Elliot's backyard musical creations. We pretended that one of his waterfalls was the sewer deep in the bowels of New York City in which Splinter and the turtles made their subterranean home. When Harmony and Carmella wanted to play on the swing set, we labeled them the evil Shredder's minions and chased them screaming through the gate and out of our territory.

I think I was two hours old the first time I heard it: "Life isn't fair." Along with breast milk, my mother fed me little snatches of wisdom. I might not have believed her right away, as my experience to that point was somewhat limited, except what she actually said was "Life isn't fair, Jane Venezuela White." Once I heard that ridiculous name I knew for sure that life wasn't fair. Then Mom added, "Life isn't fair, but it's good, and you're going to have a great one. I can see it in your eyes."

At least she was half right. Life isn't fair. That's why everyone needs an imaginary enemy. It's fabulous having someone to blame.

Copycat

When I was eight, we went to Texas to visit the ancient Aunt Jane my parents were so fond of—the one whose mundane name was tattooed on my birth certificate. She was awful. She had orange hair piled on top of her head, bright pink toenails, and a silky dress with big magenta flowers all over it. The whole ensemble bottomed out with a pair of neon green flip-flops stippled with teeth marks where her cocker spaniel had attacked them. She smelled like bourbon, her supply of which she and my parents managed to diminish significantly that afternoon. Aunt Jane, Mom, and Dad told stories and laughed a lot, and I was so bored that I actually played with Zander and Carmella. By choice.

Aunt Jane kept calling me her "sweet little namesake" and saying how much I looked like her. That scared me to death. She was one huge wrinkle with bones sticking out and a puff of wild hair on top. If I really looked like her, I was in for one sorry life. When I opened my mouth to protest, Mom gave me the eye and Dad elbowed me in the ribs, so I held back my denials.

When it was time to go, Mom pulled me aside and told me to give Aunt Jane a kiss. "No way," I snarled.

"Jane." Mom crossed her arms.

"She's yucky," I protested.

"She's your aunt, and she loves you, and she's a delightful person. And you, young lady, are already in enough trouble for putting frogs in her toilet. So give her a kiss, now."

I knew when I was licked. I walked up to Aunt Jane, holding my breath. I stood on tiptoe, steeled myself, and kissed her.

I survived. That's the only positive thing I can say about that kiss.

On the ride back to the hotel, Dad said, "Now, Janie, that wasn't so bad, was it?"

"I'd rather eat dead bats smothered in maggot sauce," I muttered.

Normally when I said things like that, my parents chuckled and talked about how precocious I was. Not that day. Dad actually pulled the car off the road, killed the engine, turned around, and glared at me. "I've had enough of this, Jane. You are not cute or funny. *You* are a brat."

Zander's eyes got huge when Dad said that. If I called Zander or Carmella a brat, I got punished. My eyes filled with tears. "I am not a brat, Daddy. Don't say that," I protested.

"*You* are a brat," he replied flatly. Then he turned around, started the car, and merged with the traffic. "And you will be punished for your behavior."

· · ·

But I didn't get punished back at the hotel. I swam in the pool and played in the elevator and jumped on the bed with Zander and Carmella. I thought Dad had forgotten about my punishment.

Wrong. When we got home, I caught it with both barrels. The usual lecture, followed by a mixture of restrictions and chores. Mom's usual refrain was right on target: life isn't fair.

Sharp and I were supposed to be doing our homework. Since we were in the same third-grade class, we usually worked together. The problem was this: Sharp always did his assignments, and I'd made a career of boycotting homework, so we spent more time battling than accomplishing anything. "Let's go swing," I suggested.

"After we do our spelling words."

"I hate doing alphabetical order. What's the point?"

"There isn't one, but it only takes a minute."

"You do it and I'll copy yours."

"Again?"

I didn't respond—instead I jumped from the picnic table and ran to the swing set.

"Jane, come back. You have to do this."

"You're not the teacher, Sharp." I was pumping my legs and soaring.

"We only have twenty words."

"That's twenty too many for me. Spelling's boring. There's a reason computers come with spell-check."

He ignored me, then threw down his pencil and closed his book. "I'm done."

"I'll copy yours."

"No."

"Yes." I jumped from the swing, ran to the table, and reached out to grab Sharp's work.

He snatched it away. "No. I'm sick of always letting you copy. Do your own."

"I just won't do it at all," I said smugly, tossing my head and returning to the swing set.

Soon after, Sharp went bike riding with Jazz and Zander. I dashed to the picnic table and took his loose-leaf page of neatly alphabetized words. I erased his name, replaced it with mine, and tucked the paper into my folder. Truthfully, I didn't really care whether or not I turned in the assignment, but I was mad at Sharp for not letting me copy.

The next day at school, I saw Sharp searching through his backpack when Ms. Lassiter called for homework. "Hey, Sharp," I whispered, and when he looked at me I held up *our* spelling words, all twenty of them carefully alphabetized in a column. Before he had time to respond, I marched up to the front of the room and dropped the paper onto the pile on Ms. Lassiter's table. On my way back to my seat I walked past Sharp's desk. "Next time you better let me copy."

"You're such a brat," he snarled, elbowing me.

"Sharp," Ms. Lassiter said. "Leave Jane alone. Where's your homework?"

"I can't find it," he replied, glaring in my direction.

I'd known from the start that Sharp wouldn't rat me out. We had our code. The next day, he grudgingly let me copy his homework, but not before splashing root beer all over me.

"Ten minutes till bedtime, kids," said Mom.

Carmella, Zander, and I were playing slapjack. "I still don't think it's fair that I have to go to bed at the same time as Zander and Carmella. He's only six, and she's five, and I'm eight," I protested.

"Write your congressman," droned Dad. That was his usual response to my complaints. I was probably the first kid in history to know what "Write your congressman" meant before the age of three. Not that I ever actually did it. I was loyal to Bubba, my only pen pal.

Zander slapped a jack of hearts and raked the pile of cards into his hand. "I'm winning," he bragged.

The back door slammed. Everyone looked up. "Who's that?" asked my mother as my father rose and rushed toward the kitchen. The rest of us cautiously followed him, honing our radar, curious and frightened as to who had entered our home.

"Luke," said my father, and even in that one word I could hear relief.

We crowded around Dad and stared at our half brother. His thick dark brown hair was tangled. He looked angry—his eyes flashed and his cheekbones seemed sharper than ever. He said nothing as he slid his backpack from his shoulder. It hit the floor with a thunk.

Dad looked quizzically at Luke. He'd spent the weekend with us and we hadn't expected him back so soon—it was only Monday, and late for a school night. "What's going on, son?"

Luke glanced at the rest of us. "I dunno." His voice trembled ever so slightly.

"I'll put the kids to bed," my mother said, ushering us

from the room. I heard the scraping of chairs on the kitchen tiles, so I guessed Dad and Luke were sitting at the table.

"Why's Luke here, Mom?" asked Zander.

"Luke's welcome anytime," she answered. "This is his home, too." Mom's open-hearted acceptance of Luke seemed artificial at times. I mean, he didn't *really* live there and she wasn't *really* his mother. Maybe she was afraid he'd think she was a wicked stepmother like in *Cinderella* and *Snow White*, so she treated him with deference. "Now go brush your teeth. And Zander, use toothpaste this time."

When Mom was tucking Carmella into bed, I slipped back down the hall to the kitchen. I stood in the doorway and saw Luke sweep the back of his hand over his eyes. Dad was at the counter pouring a glass of juice.

"Jane, you've been sent to bed." I jumped at my mother's voice behind me, sterner than normal.

"I want to kiss Dad goodnight," I whined.

"Go to bed *now*," Mom ordered.

Dad blew me a kiss from across the room. "Go on, Janie. Mind your mother."

Luke was in eighth grade when he moved in with us. The night he'd interrupted our game of slapjack, he'd gotten in a fight with his stepfather and run away, although I'm not sure if it really qualifies as running away when you leave your mom to go live with your dad.

Things got weird around the house for a few days. Dad was constantly on the phone. I knew he was talking to Luke's mom because I heard him say "Calm down, Sandy," and "He'll be fine, Sandy. He's thirteen years old," and stuff like that. Then he and Mom would go into their bedroom and talk in soft voices. Luke wouldn't speak to anyone—he just sat on the back steps sulking or stargazing or petting Banjo.

Then it became official and Sandy brought Luke's belongings to our house in cardboard cartons. When Luke saw her car pull into our driveway, he ran out the back door and jumped the fence. He climbed the rope ladder to the tree house nestled in one of the deMichaels' oaks. Dad helped Sandy unload Luke's stuff. Then I saw Sandy crying when she and Dad stood in the doorway talking quietly. He put his arm around her and she wept on his shoulder, but it didn't make me angry, even though my mother was alone in the kitchen cooking dinner.

At first, Luke was like a caged beast, growling and snarling. Mom said it was part of growing up and that he'd been going through a difficult time, but when his wrath was directed at me, my feelings got hurt. He was a hero of mine—the invincible older brother. The smallest sharp word or briefest derisive glance shattered me.

Luke wasn't always awful. When he caused one of us to cry, he'd apologize and try to make us laugh. Sometimes he brought me stuff . . . a pack of Starbursts or an arrowhead he found at the clay pits or a Canadian penny. He was good at art, and since he knew I loved magical creatures, he covered sheets of paper with griffins and dragons and wizards.

There was one drawback to Luke's moving in with us: Mom gave him Carmella's room, insisting he needed privacy, and moved Carmella in with me, despite my protests. I tried everything—whining, crying, arguing, sulking, and shouting—but to no avail.

"You're sharing your room with your sister and that's it," my mother said, crossing her arms.

"But Mom—"

"We'll redecorate. How about that?"

"I dunno," I mumbled. "It's still not fair."

"You can choose the paint and new bedspreads."

That was at least something.

"Purple?" Mom asked. "You mean lavender?"

"No, I mean purple. Like this." I pointed to the picture in the catalog.

"Purple comforters are fine, but let's choose something . . . softer for the walls."

"You said I could pick, and I pick purple." Naturally, I got my way. She had promised, after all. The only problem was Carmella's obsession with Barbie, which meant that the walls on her side of the room were plastered with Barbie posters, an odd contrast to the movie stills of Godzilla eating Tokyo and *Escape of MechaGodzilla* hanging on my side. Nonetheless, the comforters were perfect, with big colorful polka dots scattered on a field of Fanta Grape that matched the walls perfectly. It was totally cool at first, but over time the room came to look and feel like a giant bruise.

Dawn

B ecause I am her namesake, Aunt Jane periodically sends me gifts. Not typical gifts like clothes, books, jewelry, or toys. Odd things. When I was six she shipped me a hummingbird's nest—tiny and fragile and carefully woven from grass and dandelion fluff. In its cavity she'd placed two solid blue marbles.

For Columbus Day, she sent me a fleet of little ships made of walnut shells. The sails were rice paper skewered on toothpicks. I must be the only kid to ever get a Columbus Day present.

At a police auction, Aunt Jane outbid everyone on a stack of ancient fingerprint cards and was certain I'd be thrilled to receive them. I thumbtacked the used ones to my bedroom wall and speculated about what ghastly crimes had been committed by the people whose identities were revealed in loops and whorls of black ink. I played detective with the blank ones and fingerprinted Zander, Carmella, Luke, and the deMichael children.

Another time Aunt Jane bought a basket of sewing

stuff at a yard sale—ribbons, beads, buttons, and embroidery thread, along with a tomato-shaped pincushion studded with pins and needles. She included a step-by-step guide to embroidery stitches.

A string of origami cranes left over from a No Nukes rally arrived in a cigar box. "I'll never forget that event," she told me later. "It was the nineteen eighties and my bridge club decided we needed to be politically active. So we chose a good cause and campaigned our hearts out until Billie Maygarden got arrested. The handcuffs scratched the gold bracelet she'd inherited from her godmother and she refused to participate after that. So as a compromise we agreed to work at the homeless shelter. That's where Billie met Milton, her fourth husband. Imagine!"

Aunt Jane simply doesn't believe in trash. "Everything is useful to someone, somewhere," she wrote on the note accompanying a bear claw dangling from a leather strap. "At the swap meet, I traded a broken toaster for this, and I do believe that the gentleman who ended up with the toaster thought he'd scored a major coup." I proudly wore the black claw around my neck for months before passing it on to Chord in exchange for a stack of X-Men and Fantastic Four comics. (I later realized he got the better end of that deal.)

A package awaited me when I came home on the last day of school when I was nine. Aunt Jane's return address sticker was plastered in the top left corner. I tore away the brown paper wrapping. Beneath it was a corrugated cardboard box embellished with paint, rhinestones, and glitter.

"What in the world?" I muttered as I opened the box. I dumped its contents on the table. Out tumbled a pile of large plastic dinosaurs and a plain white envelope with "Sweet Jane" written on the front. (Aunt Jane always called me Sweet Jane because of some Lou Reed song from the nineteen seventies.)

"Way cool," said Zander, standing beside me. These weren't regular plastic prehistoric reptiles. They'd been dressed and decorated. Painted and pierced and bejeweled. T. rex sported a black Mohawk, bulky brass zippers, and heavy chains. Stegosaurus was clad in black leather duds with numerous piercings in his armor plates. His claws were painted crimson. Triceratops was tattooed with a skull and crossbones. Silver hoops adorned his faceplates and eyelids. Black and white stripes ringed his thick tail. Chrome hose clamps circled Brontosaurus's long neck. Large black and red anarchy symbols were painted on his massive torso in what looked like fingernail polish.

"Aunt Jane is so weird," I said, tearing open the envelope.

Sweet Jane,
    Some teenagers were selling these at the craft fair and they were the cutest things I'd ever seen. I immediately thought of you. The kids who made them called them Gothosaurs. Isn't that clever? I hope you enjoy them.

                                Love,
                                Aunt Jane

"I wish she'd send me great stuff like this. Mom and Dad should've named me Jane," said Zander.

I laughed. "Yeah, right. You're a guy, remember?"

I gathered up my Gothosaurs and arranged them on the shelf above my bed. I had to admit, they were awesome.

Sharp thought it was a great idea. Naturally, because it was *his* idea. And it did seem like a good idea at the time (at least to a pair of nine-year-olds). A magical idea. One that would make this party shine brighter than all others. He swore me to secrecy. As usual, I fell in. If Sharp was Batman, I was Robin. If he was Scooby Doo, I was Shaggy. If he was Tarzan, I was Jane. . . . Well, I *am* Jane, so that one doesn't really count. It seemed harmless enough, though, and wouldn't everyone be charmed and surprised at Peggy's celebration?

Every year at the summer solstice, Peggy deMichael threw a party. It was a large affair with crowds of people, plenty of food and drinks, beautiful decorations, musical entertainment provided by Elliot and his friends, and games for the children. It was a tradition we all looked forward to.

The entire week before the party was devoted to preparations. The deMichael kids polished furniture and scrubbed bathrooms. They dusted and vacuumed and washed windows. Their kitchen was heaped with ingredients, dirty dishes, and platters of hors d'oeuvres. You didn't dare enter or you'd risk being conscripted to grate cheese or peel potatoes.

In most households, it's the Christmas decorations

that get broken out once a year. At the deMichaels', it was the lawn mower. That summer I watched from the shade of the patio as Sharp and Chord took turns forcing the rusted mower through the grass. It whined in mechanical protest as it chewed at the thick lawn, and stalled out every few feet. The first time I heard either of them cuss was during one of their annual yard-grooming adventures. I was shocked at the number of forbidden words they knew.

It was the night before the party. Sharp and I met in the deMichaels' backyard after dark. He was armed with a large bottle of Dawn dishwashing liquid. "Let's start here," Sharp suggested in a whisper, and I followed him to the largest of Elliot's fountains, the one in whose pool floated the pizza-sized water lilies my mother always admired. The edges of the bright green leaves curled toward the sky to keep pond water from pooling in them. Their creamy white and buttery yellow blossoms seemed to glow in the darkness. Sharp stood at the spillway and poured Dawn into the stream of water. Within seconds bubbles began to form. "Perfect," he whispered. "It's gonna be fabulous."

We went to a waterfall made from a series of flat stones forming a ragged tower. They were covered in a carpet of fuzzy green moss. I took the liquid from Sharp and squeezed it onto the highest stone. We smiled as the cascading water bubbled and foamed.

"We still have almost half a bottle," Sharp said when we'd soaped the last of Elliot's waterworks. "Might as well finish it off."

We emptied Dawn into pools and ponds already foamy and white.

"Peggy's gonna love it," said Sharp. The deMichael

kids all called their parents Mom and Dad when addressing them but Peggy and Elliot when referring to them in conversation. "I can't wait till tomorrow."

"Elliot's raging," said Luke the following morning when he walked into the kitchen with the newspaper. He grabbed an apple from the fruit bowl and polished it on his T-shirt.

Mom looked up from her coffee. "About what?" Elliot, very even-tempered, seldom raged.

"Bubbles." Luke looked at me as he bit into his apple with a loud crunch.

"How could Elliot be mad about bubbles? Everyone likes bubbles," said my mother.

Again Luke stared at me. "*Someone* put soap in all of his ponds. There are bubbles everywhere. It's like a washateria gone insane. Wait till you see the water lilies. They're wilted and slimy. What a mess."

I went to the window. Elliot squatted in his backyard, siphoning water from a shallow pond with the garden hose. It shocked me to see the waxy flowers all brown and shriveled, half buried in dirty gray foam. Luke stood beside me. "The mosses'll die, too, and the grasses in the little pond at the back fence. And all the rest. Elliot said the soap will kill everything."

"I'm going outside," I said.

All the deMichael children except Chord were at work around the property. I cautiously approached Sharp, who was filling the wheelbarrow with dead plants. "Does he know who did it?" I whispered.

"Yeah, he knows."

My stomach lurched. "Who told him? Chord? That rat. Where is he?"

"I don't know where he is. You know how he does that disappearing act when we have chores to do." Sharp sighed. "But it wasn't Chord. I left my shoes on the patio."

"That's not evidence."

"The empty Dawn bottle was with them."

"Why'd you do a dumb thing like that?"

"It wasn't on purpose," he said defensively. He heaped one last armload of dead plant matter into the wheelbarrow. "Besides. I didn't think *this* would happen. I thought it would be beautiful."

I followed him across the yard to the compost heap. "My parents are going to barbeque me," I moaned, imagining how beserk my parents would go when they discovered my role in the destruction of Elliot's gardens. The lectures and punishments. The restrictions. I hated the idea of summer vacation ending in June. "I'm cooked."

Sharp dumped the wheelbarrow load and turned to glare at me. "*Your* shoes weren't there. No one knows about you," he said.

"Yet."

"I'm not a snitch. I won't tell."

I didn't believe him in spite of our code. This was big. Too much for one person to bear the responsibility for.

By evening, all the bubbles were gone. The waterworks looked sterile. Their flowers and grasses had been stripped away and thrown on the compost heap. The mosses carpeting the stones had turned a dull muddy color. When I stood near them, the smell of rotting vegetation assaulted me.

The rest of the yard looked festive. Strings of Japanese lanterns were stretched between the trees. Tiny white lights were twined around the trunks and into the fronds of the palms. Mason jars half-filled with sand flickered with tea-light candles on the tables. Wreaths of fern and baby's breath circled the jars.

I looked around for Sharp, wondering if he was angry with me. Then Chord walked up. "Where's Sharp?" I asked.

"You won't be seeing his face for a good long time. Jazz and I are smuggling in bread and water."

"Is he coming to the party?"

"No way. He's not allowed to leave his room 'cept to go to the bathroom. And he has to do yard work all summer. Elliot says he needs to learn to appreciate the balance of nature."

I looked up at the second-story window of what I knew to be the bedroom Sharp shared with Jazz and Chord. Light was spilling through the glass. I wondered what Sharp was doing. . . . Reading, practicing an instrument, seething?

I glanced across the patio at Elliot and my father, engaged in an intense conversation. Certain that Dad was learning of my part in Elliot's backyard environmental disaster, I knew I'd soon be in as much trouble as Sharp. I decided to visit the food table and fuel up before I got evicted, or imprisoned, or entombed, or whatever. I took my plate to the farthest corner of the yard, where there was an arbor with two benches and a small pond. The structure was made of gray limbs that were long and straight, with the bark and smaller branches stripped away. Elliot had built it years ago from the remains of a tree that had snapped during a hurricane.

I sat on the bench. The sweetness of the jasmine climbing the arbor mingled with the pleasing aromas wafting from my plate of food. I suddenly wondered if the koi that usually swam in the pond had survived our crime. I began to eat. I wasn't exactly gluttonous, but maybe filling my stomach would displace the guilt lingering inside me. Was it my fault Sharp had been stupid enough to tattle on himself? I absently tossed a crust of bread into the little pond. Had the soap killed Elliot's fish? I gazed into the water but saw no movement, only the vaguest reflection of my own face—but it was dark, after all. They *had* to be in there, with their lovely, nearly translucent tails spreading behind them.

The wind chimes hanging from the arbor tinkled and I looked up at the house. Sharp stood in the window, the light behind him illuminating his hair like a halo. A halo? Or was that my guilt again? I popped a shrimp into my mouth but it stuck in my throat. I felt an unreasonable, ridiculous urge to confess—to go to Elliot and beg his forgiveness. I took a sip of punch to wash down the shrimp. Why should I fess up just because Sharp did? Is it my fault he's so stupid? I asked myself defensively as I bit into a cheese straw. He knew what was at stake. He should have kept his big mouth shut.

Sharp's silhouette left the window. I saw him cross to the doorway, where the light switch was mounted, and then the room went dark. I imagined him lying on his back staring at the ceiling, furious with me.

Luke, now almost fifteen, sat down on the bench across from me with his long legs sprawled out in front of him. "So, Janie, you're letting Sharp take the heat all alone?" he asked. Luke and my father were the only two people on the planet who got away with calling me Janie. Sometimes Chord or Zander taunted me with that nickname, but I always made them pay. Zander I'd just beat up, since I was bigger than he was, but Chord I rewarded with a squeeze-and-twist pinch that left an angry purple mark tattooed on his forearm.

I pretended confusion. "What are you talking about?"

"Elliot's gardens."

"Sharp was really dumb to do that," I said casually.

"Yeah. But now he's busted and you're in the clear. Don't you feel guilty?"

"Why should I?" I responded defiantly. I refused to meet his eyes though I could feel them on my face.

"I saw you, Janie."

"Saw me what?"

"Saw you with the dishwashing soap. You and Sharp together. Course I didn't know what you were doing . . . just thought it was another of your goofy games. I was sitting on the back porch with Banjo."

I raked my fork across the plate. "Mind your own business," I muttered.

"Peggy told Dad it'll take years to replace those plants. And Elliot's been babying them forever."

"Plants die."

"Those had a little help. A lot, actually."

"Shut up, Luke. I didn't do anything."

"It'll be expensive, too, to replace them. Apparently plants cost a lot. Specially water lilies and stuff like that."

"Bug off," I snapped.

"Your dirty little secret's safe with me," he said, walking away.

My plate was empty. My stomach was full. But I didn't feel satisfied. I felt something else—something uncomfortable that I wanted to avoid. Something that made me turn away from the mirror when I went indoors to use the bathroom. It made me glad that, because of his punishment, I wouldn't have to face Sharp for a while.

> Dear Bubba,
>   Is it my fault Sharp was so stupid as to leave evidence of his crime? I was smart enough to erase all traces of my involvement, and he should have done the same. Someone that clueless deserves to get caught.
>
>   In the clear,
>   Gabriel

I Spy

Sharp sat beside me and smiled. "Elliot's right."

"About what?"

"Water."

I looked at him as if he was speaking Sanskrit. His face was serious and his tone of voice indicated that he believed this information was of extreme importance. He patiently explained that he'd spent several weeks carefully listening and observing. "Elliot says faucet water and nature water sound different. Since a sprinkler is a machine, it has a constant rhythm. You can alter the rhythm by changing the water pressure or adjusting the settings, but its rhythm is still a static thing.

"But rain rhythms are controlled by the energies of the universe—by wind and the earth's rotation and the size of the water droplets, stuff like that. And it can change from instant to instant. It's much more lyrical. Much freer.

"The same goes for running water. The faucet produces a constant flow, but a river slips and slides to the sea at a rate that changes with every stone or curve."

"You're weird," I said.

"But you get it, don't you? And it makes perfect sense."

"You're weird," I repeated.

But I did get it, and it did make sense. I just wondered why normal people would worry about such things. Sometimes I was frightened by Sharp's ideas and his assumption that other people pondered the same bizarre stuff he did.

"Jazz and Zander were wrestling in the house," said Carmella, hands on her hips and head cocked slightly to the side. "That's against the rules."

"And Banjo was going crazy," added Harmony. "Running in circles and barking like mad."

"They knocked Mom's African violet off the table."

"We saw them."

"There was dirt all over the place."

"Then they stuffed the plant back in the pot, but it's all smashed looking. It's a mess like you wouldn't believe." Carmella looked smug.

"Wait till your parents see it." Harmony shook her head.

"Guess what else?" said Carmella.

I looked at the two six-year-old tattlers and said nothing.

"You won't believe it," she added, hoping to suck me into their psychotic game.

Still I didn't reply.

Harmony and Carmella leaned close to me, like we were all coconspirators in the same secret plot. "The Blackshires' dog got picked up by the dogcatcher," reported Carmella.

Mr. Blackshire and his son, Jason, a classmate of Carmella and Harmony's, lived in the green house on the corner.

"So?" I responded.

"You wanna know why?"

"Not really, but I'm sure you're going to tell me."

"Jason forgot to close the gate, and Tag got away, and Mrs. Thomson called the dogcatcher because Tag dug up her tomato plants."

Harmony joined in. "Jason has to do jobs to help pay the fine. We heard Mr. Blackshire say so. He's gotta rake the yard and wash the car and stuff."

"He's really mad at Mrs. Thomson. Calls her the mustard witch because of that yucky jogging suit she always wears."

"Tell me . . . do you two little snoops report my private happenings to everyone else?"

"Oh no," said Carmella as she and Harmony shook their heads, but they looked as guilty as cats pawing at a fishbowl.

The Meltdown

Until the spring of my fifth-grade year, my family lived an existence you might see on a black-and-white television sitcom from the days of *Leave It to Beaver*. Things around my house were structured and routine for the most part. Dad went to work at the insurance company. Mom went to work at the optometrist's office. Sometimes we'd go out to dinner on the weekend, or pack a picnic lunch and go fishing, or rent some movies. Whatever. We watched the World Series in October. We went to the Christmas parade the second Saturday in December. We attended Uncle Grayson's annual Fourth of July barbeque and the deMichaels' yearly summer solstice bash. Occasionally, we played a game of cards or Monopoly. Typical suburban family living the typical suburban life. Dull and reliable, but safe. No surgeon general's warnings needed to be attached. No disclaimers. No fine print. We thought our lives were great.

Then Dad had the Meltdown.

Before the Meltdown, Dad was as predictable as the

tides. He'd come home from work in the evening, give us all kisses, trade his suit and tie for jeans, and sit on the sofa in the family room to watch the news. We'd eat dinner, after which he'd help Mom with the dishes before wandering back to the TV, where he'd watch a crime drama or maybe a documentary, switching to the Weather Channel occasionally to see what conditions were predicted for the rest of the week. Sometimes his eyes would go glassy as he sighed to my mother, "It'll be good fishing tomorrow . . . and it's cobia season. Wish I didn't have to go to work." Later he'd send us off to bed with a goodnight kiss. Sometimes from my bedroom I'd hear him click the television off and open the front door. That usually meant he was stargazing.

Then one afternoon, Dad came home from work with a box of black plastic garbage bags in one hand and a bottle of Captain Morgan Original Spiced Rum in the other. I'll always remember that label, on which a dashing dark-haired pirate stands straight and tall with a silver sword clasped in his right hand and his left leg propped on a wooden keg. His blue cape billows behind him as if caught in a salt-kissed sea breeze.

So there was Dad with the plastic bags and the bottle. And get this—he was singing "Satisfaction," that Rolling Stones classic. Dad's no Mick Jagger, but he was belting it out pretty darned good. ". . . 'cause I try, and I try, and I try . . ." He paused to take a big swig of Captain Morgan's straight from the bottle. For percussion, he beat on the box of Hefty Cinch Sak trash bags. ". . . can't get no . . . satisfaction . . ." He pulled out a Hefty bag and shook it open.

Zander, Carmella, and I followed Dad down the hall to our parents' room. ". . . useless information supposed to fire my imagination . . ." He took another hit from the bottle and flung open the closet door. The Captain Morgan's made a dull thump when he slammed it onto the closet shelf. He snatched a handful of neckties from his tie rack and stuffed them into the bag. Zander poked me in the ribs with his elbow and raised an eyebrow (but not in the totally cool way of Mrs. Perkins, my second-grade teacher). Carmella stood there gaping. ". . . can't get no . . ." Dad crammed a pile of his carefully laundered and pressed work shirts—hangers and all—into the bag. ". . . hey hey hey . . . that's what I say. . . ." He snatched the bottle of rum by the throat and tilted it to his mouth. ". . . can't get no . . ." He pulled his dress pants out of the closet and dumped them into the bag in a big wad.

"Robert?" said Mom, who'd been gardening in the backyard and had only just appeared in the doorway. Her voice was a whisper of confusion.

". . . try, and I try . . ." Dad removed another handful of shirts and a couple slipped like reluctant ghosts to the floor.

Mom stepped into the room "Robert, what are you doing?"

Dad danced over to her, a huge smile on his face. He wrapped her in his arms and planted a noisy kiss smack on her lips. Then he took another hit from that bottle. Zander, Carmella and I sat on the bed, transfixed. We'd never seen anything like this. Not at our house, anyway—maybe on some weird TV show, but this was real life. It was *our* father stuffing his clothing into trash bags and getting drunker by the minute.

"Robert!"

Dad yanked another bag from the box and sat on the closet floor. Shoe after shoe went into the bag—black ones, brown ones, shoes with laces, loafers. Shiny leather. Touches of suede. Spiraling dots punched into the uppers in fancy designs.

"Robert, what is going on?" This time my mother's voice was strong. She stepped over to the closet.

Dad looked at her and laughed hysterically, clutching his sides. Tears streamed down his face.

It was weird to sit there on my parents' bed with my father laughing and drunk on the closet floor, surrounded by the dregs of his wardrobe, while my mother stood over him. That's the only time I've ever seen my dad drunk. It was scary and exciting and amusing and embarrassing all at once.

Zander started giggling, and Carmella sat beside him, big-eyed but, for once, mute. "Jane," said my mother firmly, "take Zander and Carmella to the kitchen and make them some dinner."

I pretended not to hear her. I didn't want to miss the grand finale, whatever it might include.

A handful of belts went into the bag, the ends dangling from Dad's fist like the tails of so many lizards. ". . . no satisfaction . . ." He was now dancing as he filled the bag with his remaining clothing.

"Jane." My mother's voice held no wiggle room.

"What am I supposed to cook?" I asked petulantly.

"Whatever you want. Now go."

"C'mon," I said grouchily, grabbing Carmella's hand and dragging her from the bed. "And stop crying, you big baby. No one's done anything to you." I turned to glare at Zander, still sitting there watching the show. "You, too, *Lysander*." Afterward, I berated myself for urging him away. If he'd stayed, he could have given me a play-by-play of the events that had unfolded while I'd been rummaging around in the cabinet in search of something to feed them.

Luke came in while I was making grilled cheese sandwiches (which I've called meltdowns ever since) and canned soup. Carmella finally unlocked her jaw and cut loose. "You won't believe what happened. Dad came home with bags and he's throwing away his clothes and Mom's all bossy acting and he kept drinking right out of the bottle and—"

"Breathe, Carmella, breathe," said Luke.

"Yeah. Hush and let me tell it. You don't even know what he was drinking," I said.

"Yes, I do. He had a bottle of—"

Zander clamped his hand over her mouth and he and I explained to Luke what was unraveling in the bedroom down the hall.

Needless to say, by the next day, the whole neighborhood knew about the Meltdown. Discretion is not Carmella's strong suit.

Dad didn't go to work anymore after that. Not in the traditional sense, anyhow.

About a week later, I came home from school to find Dad and Uncle Grayson sitting at the kitchen table, which was covered with papers and brochures. Uncle Grayson's fingers were dancing on the keys of a calculator while he called out numbers and percentages that Dad scribbled in a notebook.

"What's going on?" I asked as I gulped down a glass of apple juice.

"Business," Dad replied.

"What business?" asked Zander, who stood beside me. We both knew Dad was now unemployed.

"Fishy business," answered Uncle Grayson, and he and Dad both laughed.

"Yes," said Dad with a wink. "There is definitely something fishy going on here."

Dissonance

Harmony and Carmella tumbled into the family room giggling. "We saw Luke at the park," Carmella announced.

"With a girl," added Harmony.

"He kissed her," Carmella said.

"On the mouth," Harmony cooed.

"It was so gross."

"Disgusting." Harmony stuck her finger down her throat.

I folded my arms across my chest and bored my eyes into the two little seven-year-old snoops. Finally I spoke. "If it was so gross and disgusting, why'd you watch?"

They looked at each other and shrugged. "We just did," Harmony said.

"It's not like they knew we were watching. They were sitting on the bench by the slide and we peeked through the trees," explained Carmella, as if such behavior was perfectly acceptable.

"That's rude," I said.

"Yeah," agreed Harmony. "They shouldn't be kissing in public."

I rolled my eyes. "I didn't mean Luke was rude. He's in high school. He can kiss someone if he wants. I meant you two were rude for watching."

"We can't help it if we see what we see," Carmella said.

"Spying on people is offensive."

"You're just jealous 'cause you missed out," taunted Carmella.

"Yeah." Harmony nodded.

"Right. Like I've never seen anyone kiss."

"We just won't tell you next time something juicy happens if that's the way you're gonna act," threatened Carmella.

"Yeah, we just won't tell you," echoed Harmony.

"You're breaking my heart," I replied.

They stomped across the room and into the kitchen, where they described, in very loud voices, everything that had transpired at the park. "I thought you weren't going to tell me," I called.

"We aren't talking to you," Carmella yelled back.

"Oh brother," I moaned, and grabbed the remote to raise the volume on the television.

I guess having a Meltdown causes adults to make all kinds of irrational decisions regarding other people. My parents did exactly that. Concerning me.

After what Mom described as an excessive number of parent-teacher conferences addressing some minor behavioral incidents at school, the household corporate giants held a board meeting. I wasn't invited until the end, when I was informed that they were tired of my troublemaking and believed that the discipline of music lessons might settle me down. "Then maybe middle school will be easier on you next year . . . or at least on us," said my mother with a sigh.

"And," added my father, "it will give you something special in your life. Something spiritually and emotionally enriching."

"Put your pajamas on, you're dreaming," I said loftily. "I'm not taking music lessons."

But Mom said, "Jane, watch your smart mouth."

And Dad said, "It has been decided. I've already spoken to Elliot, who said he'd be delighted to take you on as a student."

"You want me to take lessons from Elliot? What instrument am I going to play? Raindrops? Buffalo bones?'"

"The mouth, Jane. Watch the mouth." I rolled my eyes at my mother's warning.

"Elliot has a guitar you can use. Your first lesson is tomorrow at nine. In the morning."

"But Dad, it's spring break," I protested. "I'm sleeping late." I never went in for that "early bird gets the worm" thing. Who'd want a worm anyhow?

"Nine a.m. And you will be required to practice every day."

"Dad," I whined.

"That's all. Please go feed Banjo, Jane."

> Dear Bubba,
>   Guitar lessons? Please! Who would design an instrument with six strings when hands only have five fingers? There is no mathematical logic to it.
>   Do re mi,
>   Gabriel

"This is a really bad idea. I'm far too lazy to play an instrument," I told Elliot.

He laughed. "I've got four lazy kids, and they can all play at least one instrument."

"But I'm *much* lazier than any of them," I said proudly. I saw Chord and Sharp lingering in the doorway. "Right, guys?"

"She's probably too dumb to catch on," Chord said.

"Yeah," agreed Sharp. "She's pretty thick. I bet she'll never learn to read music. She can barely read our science book."

"I am not dumb, and I can too read the stupid science book," I snapped. I turned to Elliot. "Let's do it."

"Take off, boys," Elliot said, and I thought I saw him wink at them. He picked up an amber-colored guitar with a rosewood neck. "Now, this is called the body, and this is the sound hole," he told me, and continued identifying all of the parts of the instrument. Then he named the strings. "It's easy to remember their names. E-B-G-D-A-E. Every Bunny Gets Drunk At Easter."

I laughed. "Maybe this won't be so awful after all."

"I'm going out to the country to set up some equipment," Elliot said. Chord, Sharp, Zander, Jazz, and I were shooting hoops in his driveway, and Elliot was shoving some recording stuff into the back of his van. "I'm going to need your help, boys," he told his sons. Then he looked at Zander and me. "If you two want to come along, check with your parents."

A few minutes later we were driving down the highway. "So where exactly are we going, Dad?" Chord asked.

"Stanfield's blueberry farm out near Deerfoot Landing."

"To pick blueberries?"

"Maybe. If we have time. I'm wiring the beehives for sound."

"You're what?" I asked, astonished.

"I'm recording the symphonies of the bees," said Elliot, smiling.

"But what if you get stung?" I asked.

"Forget that! What if *we* get stung?" asked Chord. "No wonder you wouldn't reveal our mission until you had successfully kidnapped us."

Elliot laughed. "We probably won't get stung. The farmers know how to handle the bees. They're quite friendly, actually."

"The farmers?" asked Jazz.

"I meant the bees, but the farmers are friendly, too."

"Yeah, right," said Chord.

I elbowed Sharp in the ribs. "Your dad's way over the edge," I whispered.

Sharp laughed. "He's still a long way from the edge, Jane," he said, and then I remembered Sharp telling me about sitting beneath the sprinkler to compare real rain to artificial rain, and I decided Sharp didn't even know where the edge was.

Chord, Zander, and I watched from afar as Elliot, the farmers, Sharp, and Jazz did that Watergate thing to the beehives. Chord stubbornly refused to get near the hives, and Elliot barred Zander and me from helping (not that I would have anyway) because he didn't want to be responsible if we got mixed up with any angry honeybees. Zander kept making annoying buzzing sounds while Chord poked me with sticks, pretending they were stingers. "You two are getting on my last nerve," I warned, but they only laughed. We returned home hours later, laden with blueberries and honey, and, in Sharp's case, three bee stings.

Elliot told me to practice guitar every day, saying that was the only way to master a musical instrument. The first week, I did. My fingertips got sore.

The next week I decided that holding the guitar counted as practice. I did strum it some but found that reading the notes slowed me down, so I ad-libbed.

The third week, opening the instrument case qualified as practice in my book. I did that every day. And I actually removed the guitar from the case twice (with some strong urging from Mom).

"I'm so proud of you for practicing without being told," Dad said one rainy Saturday. "You're sounding better all the time."

"Thanks," I replied, desperate to hide my confusion. I'd spent the whole morning playing video games.

"Elliot said you were progressing slowly. I'm not sure I agree. I'm no musician, but what you did today is a vast improvement over last week."

"Thanks." What in the world was he talking about? I hadn't touched that guitar. I hated it! My fingers got tangled in the strings, and after a month of lessons I still couldn't read the notes. All that line, space, sharp, flat, and eighth-note stuff rattled my brain. It amazed me when I saw Sharp and Chord brush their fingers effortlessly over the strings to fill the air with music. When I played, it sounded more like a train wreck.

Ferrier's Point Marina

One morning about seven weeks after the Meltdown, Dad said, "Go put on your shoes and socks. I'm taking you kids to meet my new girlfriend."

The feeling inside me was horrible. I wanted to find a place to hide and never return, to scream, puke, rage, and die all at one. I knew my mother was Dad's second wife, that we were his second family—my half brother Luke made that obvious. Was Dad now moving on to some other lady? I looked at my mother, who was loading the dishwasher. Her face was placid and undisturbed—almost satisfied.

"Girlfriend?" asked Zander. "You can't have a girlfriend. Mom's your girlfriend."

Dad winked. "That she is."

"Well, you can't have another one," argued Zander.

"Just go put on your shoes," said Dad. "Now."

I grabbed Luke's elbow in the hallway. "Dad has a girlfriend?"

Luke, stonefaced, shook me off without comment.

Minutes later, we were all piling into the car. And when I say "all," that includes my mother. I knew some kids from school who had unusual family setups, so a list of creative possibilities raced through my head. At the same time, it simply did not compute—we were a *regular* family, and it made no sense for my mother to sit in the car smiling while my father took us to meet his girlfriend.

The morning sun streamed through the car windows and into my eyes, making tears slip from them. I turned my face to the side so no one could see.

Dad pulled into the parking lot at Ferrier's Point Marina on Bayou Angelica and parked. "Come on," he said. Reluctantly, I unlatched my seatbelt. I didn't want to leave the comparative safety of the car. As long as we sat there, nothing could change. "Can't wait for you kids to see her. She's a real beauty."

Again I looked at my mother—tried to read hurt or shame or anger in her eyes, but again she seemed more content than she had since the day of the Meltdown.

We followed them down the pier. Oddly, they were holding hands. Dad stopped in front of a cabin cruiser with teak trim. "Well?"

Luke, Zander, Carmella, and I stood by mute.

"What do you think?" Dad asked. "Isn't she gorgeous?"

I looked around. We were the only people on the dock.

"Who?" Zander asked, at least as confused as I was.

My father grinned. "My girlfriend. *Annika Elise*."

Luke and I exchanged glances. I knew that Luke, like me, was wondering if this was Meltdown Number Two and we'd be heading for the loony bin with Dad in a straitjacket before the day ended. "There's no one there," Luke muttered uncomfortably.

Dad grinned. "The boat, kids. People commonly refer to a boat as 'she.'" He motioned toward the words *Annika Elise* painted on the stern in blue and silver letters. I hadn't noticed them before when I was scanning the piers for some supermodel of a woman.

"Boat?" Carmella asked.

"This is the girlfriend?" I asked.

"Yeah. She's perfect," Dad said dreamily. "Course, I can't afford her right now, but one day—"

That's when I hauled off and punched him as hard as I could right in the stomach and fell to the pier sobbing loudly.

It amazes me how clueless parents can be at times. Mine were shocked to discover what I'd been imagining as we drove from our house to Ferrier's Point Marina. Shocked to find I'd believed there was some glamorous lady lurking in the shadows of our family dynamics.

When things settled down, Dad led us to a picnic table at the foot of the pier. "The real reason I brought you here was to share some news with you. Uncle Grayson and I have leased Ferrier's Point Marina, and I'm going to manage it."

I looked around. The grounds were somewhat overgrown, and many of the piers showed signs of neglect. Paint peeled from the sides of the three buildings on the property, and weeds poked their heads and arms through the oyster-shell parking lot. Scraps of paper, old beer cans, and fast-food wrappers were trapped in the saw grass and reeds lining the banks. All that aside, the place had potential. It was certainly a lot more appealing than the insurance company offices in the big glass building downtown.

Incidentally, Dad doesn't call his transformation a Meltdown. That's just my name for it. He doesn't call it a midlife crisis, either, like Mom's sister does. He calls it his mid-death crisis. Said he was dying more and more every day until he threw away his insurance company clothes and resuscitated himself. He claims he'll never again own a piece of clothing that requires dry-cleaning or ironing.

Schooled

Zander, Carmella, and I spent nearly every day that summer at the marina. When Luke wasn't at his mother's (he spent alternate weekends with her), he was usually there as well, but he was just as likely to spend the day organizing a corner of the workshop, replacing broken decking, or painting as he was to hang out with us. Occasionally boat owners hired him to detail their boats, and he always called us over to admire his work when a job was completed.

The place was vast, with a large area for parking boat trailers, a store/office, a workshop, and a windowless building crammed with miscellaneous junk—some nautical, some as out of place as a battered '67 Chevy Malibu, a crib, a rotted-out upright piano, and a dented airplane propeller. Playing in that overstuffed building was the treasure hunt of the century for us, and we were heartbroken the day Dad and Uncle Grayson decided to clear it out to turn it into a bait shed.

The main building was two stories, with office space

upstairs and a general store on the bottom floor. The inventory was minimal, mostly whatever some desperate boater might have forgotten to pack—bread, peanut butter, Vienna sausage, and the like. Cigarettes, sunscreen, sunglasses, batteries, and similar high-priority items were shelved beside the cash register. Peg-Boards on the back wall held fishing tackle, life jackets, and basic emergency repair supplies. A pyramid of propane tanks, popular with the live-aboards, was stacked next to the beer cooler. Then there was the section that Uncle Grayson sarcastically called "The Boutique," where T-shirts, flip-flops, beach towels, and hats were on display. A couple of ancient pinball machines were jammed into the corner, and Dad and Uncle Grayson hung a dartboard on the wall. On rainy or slow days, they'd have lengthy dart tournaments. A chart tacked to the wall recorded their wins and losses.

The back room was a kitchen outfitted for only the most basic meals. It held a fryer, a stove, a fridge, and counters topped with open shelves. Uncle Grayson had dreams of upgrading the facility enough to one day open a restaurant on the property, but that was a long-term goal. For the time being, the kitchen was only used by employees and family.

The piers were the main attraction for us kids. We spent hours on them. We fished and skipped rocks in the bayou. Played pirate or hide-and-seek. Raced our bikes up and down the driveway, boardwalks, and boat launch. Our favorite game, until a gash in Carmella's forearm that required six stitches caused Dad to ban it, was a modified version of king of the mountain where the goal was to toss your opponent overboard.

I grew to love that place—it represented a freedom we'd never experienced. We could go barefoot all day, eat when we chose, and get as dirty as we pleased. The rules were vague and only enforced when issues of property rights or safety surfaced.

Sharp and I were draped across branches of one of the oaks in the deMichaels' backyard. It was late afternoon, and insects buzzed in the air around us. We were playing hailstorm, one of our favorite made-up games. After setting a five-gallon bucket beneath the tree, we filled our pockets with pebbles and climbed into the branches. Then we took turns trying to drop rocks into the bucket. "That's eight for me," said Sharp when I heard his stone hit the plastic bottom.

I'd spent so much time at the marina that summer that I'd barely seen the deMichaels, at least compared to previous summers. School started in two weeks, and then things would really change. All through fifth grade, teachers and parents had lectured us on how different middle school would be.

"Are you nervous about sixth grade?" I asked as I dropped my pebble. It bounced on a lower branch and ricocheted at an odd angle away from the pail.

"No."

"Not at all?"

"No." His stone landed about three inches from the bucket.

"But middle school's different than elementary."

"I'm not going."

I laughed, remembering how Sharp had insisted he

wasn't going to go to kindergarten when we were five. "You have to go, Sharp."

"No, I don't. I'm staying home."

"It's the law, airhead." My pebble nailed the target. "That makes seven."

"No, I don't. Elliot's going to teach Chord and me. We'll be homeschooled."

"No way."

"Yes way. I thought I told you. . . . Nine," he said when his rock hit the pail's rim and bounced in.

"No."

"Well, Chord didn't do so great last year at Kingston Middle, and he got in trouble a lot, so last week Peggy and Elliot decided we'd learn more at home."

I pondered this bit of news. Sharp and I had always gone to school together; often we were even in the same class. I dropped three stones at once, breaking the rules. None of them scored me a win. The idea of starting middle school without Sharp was unsettling. I'd assumed we'd help each other through the early weeks until we got the hang of things. "Wouldn't you rather go to real school?" I asked.

"No. Elliot's planning lots of fun stuff for us to do. I think it'll be great."

"But *everyone* goes to school," I insisted.

"Lots of kids are homeschooled, Jane. It's not that weird."

"It's your turn," I said moodily. I didn't like this new situation and refused to discuss it further.

Sharp dropped a pebble and scored another point. "Ten."

Mom and Dad were in the kitchen, and Carmella and I were watching cartoons in the adjacent family room. "Doesn't Jane sound good? I think music lessons were a great idea," I heard Mom say.

"So do I. She needed something like that."

"She's picking it up quickly. Elliot thinks she's not doing so well, but he's used to his own kids, who've been exposed to music forever, and probably had a genetic head start as well."

"Just listen to her. She sounds quite fluid for a beginner," Dad said. I could hear some guitar riffs drifting down the hall.

Carmella looked at me. "What are they talking about?"

"Who knows? They must be hearing the radio. Change to channel seven. Bugs Bunny is on."

"Jane?" I heard a confused voice in the doorway.

"Hi, Mom," I said brightly.

"I thought you were in your room practicing."

"Nope. Watching cartoons. I'll do it later."

"But then . . . who's that?" She turned to walk down the hall. Curious, I followed her, and arrived at my room just in time to see her open the door and gawk at Zander, who was sitting on my bed with the guitar in his arms. "Zander?"

He looked up. "Hi, Mom."

"You're playing Jane's guitar?"

"Yeah. She wasn't using it. I'm just fooling around."

Mom looked at me. Then she looked at Zander. Then back at me. "Zander, give your sister the guitar. Jane, play."

Zander handed me the instrument. I sat on the bed and tried to strum something that just might have been able to disguise itself as music. "You're holding it wrong," Zander whispered, and he adjusted the guitar in my arms just like Elliot always did during my lessons.

I stumbled over the strings, twanging and twinging and twonging, and then I set the guitar aside in defeat. "Mom, I can't do this," I said. "It's too complicated."

She sighed. "Let's go talk to Elliot. You too, Zander."

So Zander played for Elliot, who was highly impressed, and then Elliot politely said to Mom, "Maybe visual art would be the right outlet for Jane. It's very spatial and concrete."

So that was the end of guitar lessons for me. (Zander took my place in Elliot's studio, only to become a star student.) And after a few months of private lessons, all I knew about the guitar was the order of the strings: E-B-G-D-A-E. Every Bunny Gets Drunk At Easter.

Flags

I was petrified the first day of middle school, but I didn't tell anyone. Instead, I relied on bravado when I headed for the bus stop. I growled at Sharp when I passed his house, but I doubt he heard me, since he was probably still trapped in his "sleeping late, I'm not going to real school" dreams. Unreasonably, I was angry with him about the whole homeschooling thing, even though it was out of his control.

I was worried about how people at Kingston Middle would react to me. I wasn't a brainiac. I knew that the teachers wouldn't show much interest in or curiosity about my progress. I'd never found myself honored with the dubious title of teacher's pet.

I wasn't one of those glamour queens with great hair and a movie-star body. My freckles made me look like a little kid. Everyone called me a tomboy, since I'd always roamed the neighborhood with Sharp, Chord, Jazz, and Zander. I had never been very interested in dolls or playing house. I didn't much like to wear dresses, either, especially frilly ones.

Sometimes, though, when no one was paying attention, I'd watch the girly girls and wish I was like them. Even in faded jeans and old T-shirts, they were beautiful and feminine. I wondered how to be like that—how to lose my clumsy mannerisms and exude graceful confidence. But I was afraid to try. Afraid people would laugh at me.

I survived the first day, the first week, and so on, until going to middle school seemed as normal as tying my shoe. Not that I was the toast of Kingston. There were times when I felt awkward trying to fit in, to find my place in that ocean of preadolescents. I learned to laugh at the appropriate times by mimicking the popular kids and hoped no one noticed if I was out of sync with the crowd. And of course, my time-tested recipe for survival served me well— a measure of slackerism, a dash of sarcasm, and a pinch of insolence. Stir well. Sprinkle in a little denial and irresponsibility. Serving size determined according to appetite.

I made friends easily, probably because I was spontaneous and average, which didn't intimidate people. It's the quiet ones kids are unsure about. I didn't immediately latch on to one friend but ran with a group of people that shrank and grew as social dynamics changed.

The major difference between elementary and middle school was the social scene. It was much more important in sixth grade than it had been the previous year. How you dressed, the music you listened to, the kids you hung out with, the way you talked—all of those things defined you, and if you didn't fit the mold you were labeled an outcast or a freak. It was all very competitive. Very fragile, too, and scary, because one simple lapse could leave you on the periphery.

"Mr. Freeman must be insane," I said, referring to the principal of Kingston Middle.

"Well, everyone knows that," agreed Samantha. "But what inspires today's assessment of his mental capabilities?"

"He assigned Emma Graham and me to raise the flag every morning for the second grading period. He said he likes to give sixth graders responsibilities to make them feel like part of the 'school community.'"

"He loves that phrase *school community*. He must have used it fifty times at orientation," said Madison.

"Sixty-two. I counted," said Samantha. We all laughed.

"I can see him choosing Emma. . . . She's like . . . perfect. But me? He must have read someone else's folder and thought it was mine. No one ever makes me responsible for anything." Emma was striking, with Hershey's chocolate skin and clear brown eyes with thick lashes. She was one of the smartest kids in our grade. Teachers read her book reports aloud as examples of high-quality work. She never came to class late or unprepared.

"It'd be hard to mess up raising the flag, wouldn't it?" asked Madison.

"I could mess up anything. Seriously, I could."

So the next morning I met Emma at the flagpole. She had already gone to the office to check out the flag. "Hi. I'm Emma. Emma Graham."

"Yeah, I know. You did the book report on *Hoot* and the science project on prairie dogs. You're famous around here." I wondered if she caught the hint of sarcasm in my voice.

"And you're Jane, the girl who yanked down Bryan Latham's shorts in PE. That was hilarious. You're so bold!"

"Hey, Coach warned the boys not to sag. Bryan had it coming." Bryan was all-right looking but gross. He was obsessed with bodily functions and noises. He talked too much and too loudly.

Emma laughed. "Yeah. Who can play soccer in shorts that are three sizes too big?"

Suddenly, I decided maybe Emma wasn't a snob like I'd thought, just quiet. Her smile seemed genuine, and she didn't act put out to be stuck with me for the next nine weeks.

We finished raising the flag. "What's your first class?" Emma asked.

"English. Yours?"

"Math. With Ms. Connors. Hey, Jane, can I sit with you at lunch?"

"Sure, Emma. See you later."

"Middle school's a piece of cake," I told Sharp one afternoon. "It's not for the chicken-hearted, homeschooled sort, though," I added smugly. "Everyone is really cool and grown up. But you wouldn't get that, would you, safe at home every day like a preschooler?"

He laughed. "We're having fun. Going on outings and doing projects. You'd love what we're doing now. Studying celestial navigation. Researching biographies of sailors and pirates. Learning to read nautical charts to map out famous voyages and the locations of shipwrecks. We're even sewing our own jolly roger flags. Mine has the side view of a skull with cutlasses crossed behind it."

"That will do nothing to prepare you for the future," I argued.

"Since when do *you* care about the future?" Sharp asked.

"I'm very ambitious."

"Yeah? So what do you plan to do with your life?"

I knew he had my number but wasn't about to cave. I blurted the first thing that came to mind. "A doctor. I'm gonna be a doctor."

"Right. Or maybe an astronaut? How about a race car driver?"

"You make me want to barf," I said, stomping away.

"A movie star? An inventor?" he called after me. "President of the United States? God?"

I slammed the front door hard enough to rattle the windowpanes.

> Dear Bubba,
>   A doctor? Right. Why do you plant
> these stupid remarks in my head? Do you
> enjoy embarrassing me? Get off when
> people laugh at me? I wish just once
> you'd clamp my big mouth shut.
>   Ever the pest,
>   Gabriel

As the weeks passed, Emma and I became close. Though we were outwardly very different, we got along well. There were things about her that reminded me of Sharp—her easygoing attitude, her curiosity, her high expectations, and her integrity. She had no trouble admitting her flaws.

That was probably what surprised me most about Emma—the fact that she actually *had* flaws. She was such a stellar student everyone expected perfection from her, but she had as many insecurities as I did. She worried about being liked. It bothered her that she was fanatically conscientious; she just couldn't not be. That was why my slacker attitude fascinated her.

I think losing our flag-raising job liberated her a bit, even though, after the fact, she was deeply ashamed.

It never would have happened if Bryan Latham wasn't so annoying. He always picked on people, embarrassing them with crude remarks. One day in the middle of their English class, he made a comment about Emma's breasts. She was mortified. I found her crying in the bathroom between classes.

"Dry your tears," I commanded. "Don't waste your energy on him. No. What we'll do is make him pay."

"Jane, I can't do that. I'd never say something rude in front of everyone."

"There are other ways," I said. "Leave it to me."

Emma and I walked down the hall. "Wow, your room's really purple," she said, gaping in the doorway.

"Yeah. My little sister and I share a room. She chose the color," I lied. I tossed my backpack onto my bed, causing dust flecks to float in the air above my comforter—another bad choice. It looked like a box of fluorescent crayons had exploded in a neon nuclear war.

"It's pretty wild," Emma said diplomatically.

"I'm repainting it soon. I haven't yet decided what color. Got any suggestions?"

"What's your favorite color?"

"Red."

"That could be just as bad as purple," she said, falling onto my bed.

"Well, tomorrow's the big day," I said, changing the subject.

"I'm not sure we should do it, Jane."

"Emma, please. We agreed." I spread an old sheet on the floor and placed a box of markers beside it. "Come on. You're a better artist than I am." So we started working, which set our plan into action.

The next day, we didn't raise the flag. We raised a less-than-flattering portrait of Bryan Latham drawn in marker on that old sheet. In case anyone was uncertain as to who the portrait represented, his name was written on it in bold black letters.

Mr. Freeman fired us from our daily flag-raising duties, telling us we were lucky he was too tolerant to suspend us. He made us apologize to Bryan, which I did with my fingers crossed behind my back.

"It was worth it," I told Emma. "We only had six more days of that job anyhow."

"I dunno, Jane. My parents are so angry and humiliated."

"They'll get over it. Mine always do."

"Why are you all sitting here on such a beautiful day when you could be out fishing?" Dad asked. It was the third day of spring break, and Luke, Zander, and I were zoned out in front of *Godzilla vs. Megalon*. We had a collection of monster movies and never tired of them.

"We're having a Godzilla marathon today," said Zander, stuffing a handful of popcorn into his mouth.

"No, you're not. You're all going fishing with me."

"Fishing?" asked Luke.

"Yes, on my boat."

Luke and Zander jumped up, totally blocking my view of Megalon, who was shooting a bolt of lightning at Godzilla from the single horn on his head. "You got a boat?" Luke exclaimed.

"The *Annika Elise*. When I introduced you to her, I said she'd one day be mine. Now she is."

"When did you do this?" Luke asked.

"Just signed the papers. Well, what are you waiting for? Go get your gear. And don't forget hats and sunscreen."

"Man, this is awesome," called Luke as we climbed aboard. He poked his head into the cabin. "Nice. Hey, Zander, check out the fridge."

"It has a refrigerator?" Zander asked as he pushed Luke aside.

"And a stove. Like a real kitchen," I said.

"Galley," corrected Dad.

"Huh?" asked Zander.

"Galley. On a boat it's called a galley," Dad explained.

"Hey, look. Here's the bathroom," said Zander after opening a small door.

"Head," said Dad.

"What?" I was puzzled.

"On a boat you call it a head, not a bathroom," Dad said.

"So that's what you're talking about when you tell Jane to use her head?" Zander said with a sneer.

"Not usually," said Dad, but I don't think Zander and Luke heard him because they were laughing so loudly. Dad turned the key. "Just listen to that engine."

"Can I drive?" asked Zander.

"After we get out in open water," said Dad. He was beaming like his sweetest dream had come true. "By the end of the summer, all of you are going to know how to operate this vessel."

"Even Jane?" asked Zander.

"Of course."

"You'd trust her with your boat?"

I kicked Zander's ankle. "Why don't you tie the anchor around your neck and go for a swim, squab," I suggested.

Betrayal

"What's the matter?" I asked Emma, who was spending the night at my house. She was obviously upset about something.

"I blew my project for Mr. Boucher. Got a B. Knew I should've spent more time on the graphics."

"A B? You're complaining about a B? What's wrong with you?"

"Stuff like that eats at me."

"Geez, people would celebrate if I got a B. I haven't even turned mine in yet. He's giving me until Monday."

"I don't see how you can be so relaxed about it. I'd be freaking. I wish I was more like you."

"Me? No one wants to be like me."

"Things don't bother you. You laugh. You don't care."

I looked out the window across the room. "I don't always laugh," I admitted. "Or maybe I do, but I don't always want to. I just don't know what else to do. What's the alternative? Tears? Tears suck."

Emma grinned. "See. That's what I mean. You're invulnerable."

"Oh Emma, please. I'm way more vulnerable than you are."

She sighed and fell onto Carmella's bed. "I don't think so, Jane. Just more up-front."

Whatever. I pressed the Play button on my CD player. "This is my favorite song. Maybe they'll play it at the dance tonight."

What Sharp and Chord were doing at Kingston Middle School's dance I couldn't imagine. It wasn't like they went to our school or anything. And they looked freaky. Sharp's hair was crazier that ever, like a million corkscrews had burst from his brain. The faded Sex Pistols T-shirt he wore was so ancient it must have been left over from Elliot's early years. And the mailman pants with the stripe down each leg were totally geeky. Chord's fashion statement consisted of nothing but a pair of huge ragged overalls sheared off just below the knees and a pair of Top-Siders.

Chord saw me from across the gym and headed my way. "Howdy there, neighbor Jane," he said, the twang in his voice underlining his farm-boy attire. He threw his arm around my shoulders.

I smiled. My face felt like it was going to crack. "Chord," I muttered, twisting away from him. "I see you dressed for the occasion."

Sharp was now standing there. "What's up?" he asked.

"Nothing," I answered flatly. I was certain everyone was wondering who they were and what they were doing hanging around with me. "Why are you two here? You don't go to this school."

"But I did last year, and my friends wanted me to come," explained Chord. "Brought my baby brother with me." He put Sharp in a headlock and rubbed his head. Sharp laughed and pushed him away.

"Well, see ya," I said, turning to quickly join my friends.

"So who are those weird guys?" asked Madison.

"Weird is right. They're my neighbors. The whole family's strange." I glanced up and realized my voice had carried. Sharp met my eyes. I looked away.

And then he was standing beside me. "I don't know what kind of head trip you're on," Sharp whispered in my ear, "but I sure don't want a ticket." He thumped my shoulder and walked away.

After that, the dance lost all glamour and dazzle. It just felt noisy and crowded. I loved the deMichael family and regretted what I'd said. But I was afraid of what my school friends would think if I hung with them.

Cassidy

Luke started seeing a girl named Cassidy who dressed like a hippie. She got on my nerves from the get-go, laughing at every cheesy thing Zander said, acting like my mother was the empress Josephine, and shamelessly sucking up to Carmella by remarking on how cute and smart she was. Luke spent so much time with Cassidy that we rarely saw him without her hanging on his arm. He brought her to the house all the time. Mom and Dad thought that was really nice. But I didn't want her around. It was irrational: I was jealous. Maybe I felt displaced. Luke and I had always shared a special bond, and I felt she got in the way of it. Had stolen it, even.

"Since when do you play soccer?" Chord asked.

"I don't. This is my Halloween costume. I'm a soccer player."

"Creative. Daring. Risky. You're really going out on a limb," he said sarcastically.

"Funny, Chord," I replied. "I told Carmella and Harmony I'd take them trick-or-treating. Want to come with us?"

"Sharp and I are going to a party," said Chord.

"I'll go with you," said Sharp, shrugging. "Maybe I'll go to the party after. Let me get suited up."

"What in the world are *you*?" I asked when Sharp reappeared a few minutes later.

"Blue."

"Blue?"

"My favorite color. It's one of the primaries, you know." His hair was sprayed an electrifying cobalt and his face, neck, arms, torso, and hands were painted to match. He was only wearing jeans and sneakers.

"Well, you're definitely blue," I said.

He grinned. "Jazz and Zander are coming, too, okay?"

"Fine. The more, the merrier," I answered.

"We're escaped convicts," Jazz announced when he and Zander appeared in tattered stripes with handcuffs dangling from their wrists and charcoal smears on their faces.

Carmella, a medieval princess, and Harmony, who said she was Charles Darwin but could've been any bearded man in a tweed jacket, were dancing around the front yard. "Come on. Let's go," begged Carmella.

"If you don't hurry all the good candy will be gone," whined Harmony.

We made the rounds through the neighborhood, laughing and eating candy. As we turned the corner to our block, I asked Sharp, "Is that what you're wearing to the party?"

"Party?"

"With Chord?"

"He's already gone." He shrugged. "I decided to ditch. I'll just hang out here."

"What'd Chord go as?" asked Zander.

"A soccer player," said Sharp.

"Ugh!" I groaned, remembering Chord mocking my costume.

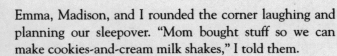

Emma, Madison, and I rounded the corner laughing and planning our sleepover. "Mom bought stuff so we can make cookies-and-cream milk shakes," I told them.

"Yum," said Emma.

"We should add some peanut butter," I suggested.

"Peanut butter? Gross. That sounds disgusting," protested Madison.

"I bet it'd be good," Emma said. "We should try it."

"Yeah. At least it'd be different," I said as we approached my house. Zander, Jazz, and Sharp were standing in the driveway attempting to juggle tennis balls but mostly just looking like fools.

"I brought a bag of chips and Samantha's bringing a big box of Nerds," said Madison.

"Speaking of nerds," I said loudly, gesturing toward the boys. Sharp was now balancing a tennis ball on his nose, while Jazz and Zander were slamming balls to the cement to see whose could bounce the highest. "Chase never acts dorky like that."

I was referring to Chase McClusky, the coolest guy in my class. I measured all other boys against Chase. None ever came close. He was handsome, slick, and very popular. I wasn't even sure he knew my name.

"Chase never acts dorky like that," squawked Zander

in a high-pitched voice. The three boys laughed. Sharp met my eyes, flipped a tennis ball into the air, caught it, and very deliberately fired it at me. "Princess Jane strikes again," he said.

"Let's get out of here," I told my friends as I deflected the incoming missile.

Cassidy stood in the doorway wearing an embroidered denim skirt, a tunic top, and a lace shawl. Red and yellow ribbons were braided into her hair. "Luke's not here," I told her.

"Where is he?"

"Who knows," I responded, although I knew he was at work at the marina, where he was Dad's right-hand man after school and on weekends. "Was he expecting you?"

"Actually, no, but there's an opening at an art show downtown I was hoping we could go to. My brother's best friend has his sculptures on display. He makes fabulous creations from glass and aluminum."

"Oh," I said disinterestedly.

"You could go with me," she suggested. "It'll be fun. They'll be serving drinks and hors d'oeuvres, and there's a band."

My brain froze. I could think of no excuse. "Sure, I guess." I grabbed my jacket and borrowed a few bucks from Zander in case I needed money.

Cassidy knew most of the people at the opening. I felt as out of place there as Sharp and Chord had looked at the Kingston Middle dance. People talked about art and music I had never heard of. When I mentioned my favorite pop star, Cassidy quickly changed the subject.

By the time she brought me home, I could grudgingly

see why Luke was attracted to her. She was captivating and quick witted. Her smile had a magnetic quality; her eyes were a warm liquid brown.

I jumped out of her car at the curb. "Thanks, Cassidy. I had a good time."

"Me too, Jane. We should hang out more often."

"Yeah, sure," I said, not really believing she'd want to spend time with me.

But once again, I was proved wrong. Cassidy started dragging me along when she ran errands for her mother or shopped for a new pair of shoes. She treated Carmella and me to the latest animated movies, saying, "Luke didn't want to go—says he doesn't like cartoons."

Cassidy was easy to talk to, and I came to share my daily victories and defeats with her—things that happened at school that I didn't discuss with Emma or my other friends if they were in any way peripherally involved. Cassidy, as a neutral party, listened and gave feedback, sympathizing at times, attempting to make me consider another viewpoint at others.

Luke was pleased that Cassidy and I had developed a friendship. He was totally fascinated with her, and expected the rest of the world to love her as much as he did. Reluctantly, I, too, grew to like her, though not with the intensity Luke felt. She became a sort of surrogate big sister, something I'd never had.

Barbie and the Little Neighbor Boys

"Let's go see what the deMichaels are doing," Zander said to me one lazy, rainy Saturday midway through seventh grade.

"You can go. I don't want to."

"Why not?"

"Those boys are boring."

"No, they're not. They're fun."

"They don't even go to real school. They're out of touch. Like you."

"No, I'm not. And how could Elliot and Peggy have out-of-touch kids? You're a snob."

"I'm too grown up to be playing with the little neighbor boys," I said in a bored voice.

"Oh yeah, you're *so* grown up," Zander said sarcastically. Seconds later, I heard the door slam.

I had nothing to do. Carmella was off somewhere with Harmony, and Luke was at work. Mom was helping Dad with the marina's budget, which meant they weren't in the mood to be disturbed. There wasn't anything worth watching on TV. Emma had joined a traveling soccer team and was in Baton Rouge for the weekend, and Madison and Samantha were at the dress rehearsal for their dance recital. So I made a break for the deMichaels' through the rain.

When Chord opened the door and Zander saw me standing there with my hair dripping, he said, "Thought you were too grown up to play with the little neighbor boys." They all laughed, so I knew that my brother, the traitor, had spilled the beans about what I'd said to him.

"Most of the 'little neighbor boys' are bigger than you, swampbreath," said Chord, giving me a scathing glare.

"And we don't want to play Barbie dolls anyway," said Sharp as he arranged cards in his hand.

"I'm not here to *play* with you losers," I lied shamelessly. "Mom sent me to tell you to come home, Zander. You need to clean your room." Then I turned around and haughtily marched down the steps and back across the yard in the rain. I stomped to my room and yanked my Bubba folder out of my backpack.

> *Dear Bubba,*
> *Those boys treat me like I'm invisible.*
> *Well, I'm not. I can see myself in the*
> *mirror. This whole thing has me staring*
> *at my hand—holding it up to the light*
> *and turning it just to make sure I'm*
> *really here. The silhouettes of my bones*

show through my flesh, so I know
I exist.

    When I was little, I saw a cartoon
on <u>Tom and Jerry</u> where a little duckling
used vanishing cream to become invisible.
Bubba, what I need is visibility cream.
Can you hook me up with some of that?
I'll share it with you if you want.
                Soggy, lonely, and bored,
                Gabriel

P.S. Just for your information, I don't
play with Barbie dolls.

I threw myself on my bed and stared at the ceiling.
The Gothosaurs Aunt Jane had sent me still sat on the
shelf over my bed. I rearranged them so that T. rex
looked like he was about to take a bite out of Brontosaurus's neck and Stegosaurus and Triceratops were
butting heads. When I rolled off my bed, my feet landed
in the large bin Carmella stored her Barbie dolls and
their accessories in. I heard the snap, crackle, and pop of
breaking plastic as my weight crushed the bright pink
Barbie sports car Carmella was so proud of. One of the
wheels popped off and flew from the bin, smacking me in
the forehead.

    Suddenly, I was inspired. I rummaged through my
backpack until I found the twenty-four-color set of
Sharpie Ultra Fine Point Permanent Markers I'd gotten
for my birthday. In the closet, I miraculously unearthed
the sewing kit Aunt Jane had given me when I was eight.

I swiped a tube of superglue from the kitchen drawer, along with an odd assortment of screws, washers, nails, thumbtacks, string, electrical tape, and the like.

"Hello, ladies," I said when I returned to my room and snatched the Barbies from Carmella's plastic bin to line them up on my bed. "Are you fashionistas ready to play Barbie makeover? Yes? Great. Who wants to go first?" I picked up a voluptuous lady clad in a sequined magenta gown. "You? Awesome. Hmmm." Holding her by the ankles, I pivoted her and evaluated her assets and flaws. "You want to go punk? No problem. We'll start with the hair."

I grabbed a purple marker and colored random strands of her platinum hair. Added some black streaks. "I think a trim is in order, don't you?" I took her silence as agreement and reached for the pinking sheers. "G.I. Joe will be delighted with your new look," I said, piercing her pert little nose with a straight pin. "But your makeup needs retouching. It's not bold enough." I uncapped the Sharpie labeled *Blue Ice* and did her lips. Outlined them in black. Then I did her eyes.

"Your clothes are all wrong," I told her. "Not to worry. It's nothing scissors and glue can't fix." I slashed and tattered and embellished. "A tattoo, I think, would complete the look." I drew a vine that snaked from her left ear to her right breast. "You're stunning," I told her as I tossed her aside. Then I chose another perky platinum-haired doll from the lineup on my bed.

Time passed. The rain finally stopped, and sunlight streamed through the windows. I stiffened the last glamour girl's hair with glue, which worked better on Barbies' artificial hair than the gel in the bathroom. "Okay, girls, we're done. You all look smashing. Absolutely smashing!" I posed all seventeen of them on Carmella's pillow.

For a nine-year-old, Carmella had quite a pair of lungs. I'll never forget her shriek when she walked into our room. It was overstated to say the least, and brought everyone running down the hall. Mom and Dad were really steamed when they saw my artistry, but Zander flashed me a covert thumbs-up, and Luke winked in my direction as he stifled a grin.

Carmella's reaction, however, went from anger to tears to despair to righteous indignation to outrage. She sobbed and threw things and stomped her feet. She yelled and screamed. She yanked one of my Godzilla posters from the wall and tore it to shreds. Threw a made-over Barbie at the shelf over my bed, causing my Gothosaurs to scatter like frightened hens. Swiped her fingernails at my face, but Dad grabbed her wrists. Calling it a temper tantrum would be like calling World War II a minor skirmish.

Have you ever noticed that judgment doesn't always rear its head until it's too late? I'll admit it. That day I didn't use good judgment. I went too far. I should have been more subtle. Pubic hair and pierced nipples were definitely overdoing it. Crossing that invisible line.

I paid the penalty, believe me. I had to work at the marina to earn enough money to replace Carmella's dolls. Dad made me wash windows, mop floors, clean bait tanks, stock fishing tackle, weed walkways, and scrub patio furniture every Saturday for weeks.

I kept the punked-out Barbies, though, somehow winning the argument that if I was buying new ones for Carmella, then the others were mine by forfeit. I lined them up on my shelf with the Gothosaurs.

Fragrance Testers

Mrs. Lezcano, my reading teacher, was a fossil with teeth the color of oatmeal and a voice even worse than fingernails dragged down a chalkboard. She gave boring lectures, making the most riveting story less exciting than junk mail. Every class period she'd also tell us about her various health issues, of which there were many. "I can't eat tomatoes or cucumbers. They give me horrendous indigestion. Keep me up all night." "I'm allergic to perfume. When I go through the cosmetics area at a department store, I have to hold my breath." "All the pollen in the air this time of year sure activates my asthma." "My migraines get worse with every episode. That new medication didn't help me one little bit."

The suck-ups and brainiacs thought Mrs. Lezcano was wonderful. She praised them, giving them perks and privileges regular kids never got, like exemptions from assignments. But the woman had disliked me from the first day of seventh grade.

Whenever she posed questions even someone of

Emma's academic ability would struggle over, Mrs. Lezcano inevitably called on me. To hide my ignorance, I answered the simplest queries with flippant responses. When we read "The Raven" by Edgar Allan Poe, Mrs. Lezcano asked, "Jane, what did the raven say?"

"Caw, caw," I said.

The class fell into hysterics, but Mrs. Lezcano went ballistic. She thrust off her ugly beige sweater and stomped across the room so that she was looming over me. "I've had more than enough of you, young lady." She sent me to the principal, charging me with the crimes of disrespect, impertinence, and brazenness. Mr. Freeman, who hadn't forgotten the Bryan Latham flagpole incident, called my parents, turning a nonevent into Kingston Middle School's private crime drama.

I chose Samantha, the most malleable of my friends, to help me implement my plan. She sat on my bed while I rummaged through the box of powdery eyes shadows, dried-out mascaras, and stubby lipsticks Aunt Jane had given me when she cleaned out her bathroom. "Found 'em," I said, putting some nearly empty perfume bottles in my backpack. "Now we're armed and dangerous."

The next day, after eating our lunches, Samantha and I slipped away to Mrs. Lezcano's classroom. I twisted the doorknob. "We're in luck. She forgot to lock up again. I swear, she's senile."

Samantha and I entered the room and closed the door. I handed her a purple glass bottle and chose for myself a clear one half full of golden liquid. "Ready. Aim. Fire," said Samantha, and we both began spritzing perfume on and around Mrs. Lezcano's desk.

"This stuff reeks," I said as the room filled with the mingled scents.

Samantha pointed to the stack of papers on the desk. "I'll sweeten these book reports," she said, saturating them.

I glanced at the clock. "We better take off. The bell's about to ring."

"She'll be a sneezing fool all through class," Samantha said, laughing.

"Let's hope it makes her itch. My neighbor Peggy gets itchy around dogs because of her allergies."

"And maybe her beady little eyes will water, too."

Samantha opened the door only to see Mr. Freeman standing in the hallway with the band director. He looked at us curiously.

"Um . . . hi . . . I was just . . . um . . . looking for my PE stuff. I thought I left it in here," Samantha explained.

"We're going to lunch," I muttered, grabbing Samantha's forearm and pulling her toward the lunchroom.

The bell rang before we reached the corner. We lingered a moment until some of our classmates preceded us; then we filed back into the classroom.

"What smells?" I heard someone ask.

"This is worse than the locker room," said another kid.

Mrs. Lezcano stood near the chalkboard wrinkling her nose. "Quiet," she squawked. "Take your seats. Now." Samantha winked at me and slid into her chair. Mrs. Lezcano grimaced. "Someone is wearing way too much perfume. Subtlety is much more effective than overstatement. And now my allergies are going to act up. You all know about the ban against fragrances in my classroom."

She launched into another bland lecture. "The

characters in this story are all unique. Jane, what makes Charlie an interesting"—cough, cough—"excuse me"—cough—"person"—cough—"ality?"

"I don't find him interesting," I said, which was true. How could a character in a story I hadn't read interest me?

I expected Mrs. Lezcano to snap at me as usual, but she didn't react. She only reached for the water bottle on her desk and sipped from it. "Now, where were we?" she said. "Oh yes, Charlie . . . He was . . ." From my seat, front and center, I could hear her breathing grow raspier. I turned to look at Samantha. She met my eyes, half amused, half afraid.

Mrs. Lezcano pulled her oversized vinyl handbag out of the desk drawer and rummaged through it. She yanked out her checkbook, wallet, and glasses case and continued digging. Her face was pale but her cheeks were red. She finally extracted an inhaler, which she latched on to. We spent the rest of the period doing vocabulary worksheets because Mrs. Lezcano told us she needed to recover.

When the bell rang, Samantha and I met at the classroom door and exchanged high fives. "A job well executed," I said.

"It went beyond our expectations. . . . The inhaler was a bonus."

"What a perfect day this has been."

"Success is the name of the game," Samantha whispered.

The following morning, things unraveled. At an after-school faculty meeting, Mr. Freeman overheard Mrs. Lezcano telling the drama teacher about her perfume-induced asthma attack. Now, he's no Sherlock Holmes, but he said he remembered Samantha and me exiting the classroom smelling like streetwalkers (he actually said that, and in front of my parents) and concluded that Mrs. Lezcano's attack was no accident.

Samantha and I were in math class when a voice on the intercom directed us to go to Mr. Freeman's office. All the other kids starting joking around, but my heart sank.

"We're screwed," I whispered to Samantha as we walked down the hall.

Through the window in the office door I saw my parents, Samantha's mother, and Mrs. Lezcano seated across from Mr. Freeman. "Oh great, they've ambushed us," I muttered.

"I can't believe this is happening," moaned Samantha.

"Let me handle things," I suggested as we entered the office.

The interrogation began. Charges were filed and the suspects named.

I tried, unsuccessfully, to convince the judge and jury that it was merely an accident. "We were getting Samantha's PE stuff, and I wanted to try out her new perfume," I said, attempting to look embarassed. "I wanted to catch a certain someone's attention."

"Give it up, Jane," my mother said. How could she be such a traitor? "We all know this was no accident."

"But—"

My father nudged me. "Jane, don't you have something you need to do?" he asked flatly.

"What?" I stage-whispered.

"You know what." He nodded toward Mrs. Lezcano.

I got the message. "I'm sorry, ma'am. We didn't know you'd get sick. I just wanted to smell girly."

Mrs. Lezcano sat there looking prim.

"Really, Mrs. Lezcano. I'm so, so sorry," simpered Samantha. I half expected her to fall on her knees and kiss Mrs. Lezcano's feet. Did she have no pride at all?

My father elbowed me again and gestured toward the principal.

"Sorry, Mr. Freeman."

"Me, too, Mr. Freeman," whined Samantha. "We aren't troublemakers. We feel awful about this. We're both sorry."

Fat lot of good it did. Samantha and I were put on three days' suspension. As I was ushered from the building sandwiched between my parents, a group of Mrs. Lezcano's favorites glared at me. Then I saw Chase, so handsome and confident, look right through me as if I wasn't there.

Dear Bubba,

Is it my fault Mrs. Lezcano is so unhealthy that a little perfume sets her off? It's not like I'm Charles Manson or Jack the Ripper. All I did was spray a little fragrance. By mistake. It could have happened to anyone. Don't think for a minute that I missed the covert glances of the other kids. Who do they think they are to ignore me?

I'm still waiting on that visibility cream. And don't blame it on the postal service, because everyone knows about FedEx.

Overnite it,
Gabriel

For the next five days (my disciplinary counseling session occurred on Friday, giving my parents the weekend plus my three-day suspension to fume), I was punished, lectured, and reprimanded. Luke, Carmella, and Zander made jabs and jokes about it, scalding me with their humor. The one comforting voice was that of Cassidy, who said middle school was a difficult time avalanched with injustices against students. "The balance of power in that environment is ridiculously skewed," she said, "and you can't expect to come out on top." I agreed with her completely. At least someone understood.

I returned to school on Thursday, expecting high fives and congratulations from my schoolmates (minus the goody-goodies). Instead, kids averted their eyes or crossed the hall when I approached. Even Mrs. Lezcano's other victims didn't appreciate the artfulness of my prank. Apparently, the rumor mill had turned a teacher's asthma attack into an act of middle school terrorism, with Mrs. Lezcano near death's door.

Samantha was mad at me, saying I dragged her into my scheme against her will. "That's not the way I remember it," I protested. "You're the one who came up with the PE clothes excuse when we saw Mr. Freeman, so don't try that innocent act with me."

> Dear Bubba,
> I've given up on that visibility cream.
> Just forget it. I'll tell you this, though—
> you make a darned good enemy. You have
> yet to come through for me in a clutch.

*Only the truest of enemies could be so
steadfast. Only the pettiest of enemies
would find pleasure in my agony. Only
the meanest of enemies could just sit back
and allow me to suffer, doing nothing.*

*Or, even worse, enjoying it. I bet you
enjoy my pain. I bet you sit there with a
bowl of popcorn and a soda, grinning
when the going gets rough. You, Bubba,
are the ultimate action hero of enemies—
the Hercules, the Incredible Hulk of
enemies. The Genghis Khan of enemies.
Well, I hope you choke on your popcorn.*

*Get a life and get out of mine,
Gabriel*

Emma kept insisting I should make a public apology. Like
I planned to stand up in front of my reading class and
openly express remorse to Mrs. Lezcano.

"Emma, I don't see what the big deal is. It was an accident."

Emma sighed. "Jane, just admit that it was a prank
gone wrong and move on."

"But it *was* an accident," I insisted. "And there's no reason for people to be giving me the cold shoulder over it."

"No one is giving you the cold shoulder. That's your
imagination."

"Emma, even you're treating me like I'm a criminal."

She laughed. "No, I'm not. I've just been preoccupied
with my research paper. Think about it, Jane. Nothing's
changed since last week except your perception. Because

you feel guilty about what happened, you're seeing things that aren't there."

"I have nothing to feel guilty about," I insisted.

"Then why'd you leave that chocolate bar on Mrs. Lezcano's desk at the end of class?"

I gaped, shocked and exposed. "What?"

"I saw you. You're not as slick as you think, Jane. But I think it was nice. Minimal, but nice."

Pins and Needles

Luke kicked my shin as he walked by, and stalked from the room.

"Hey, that hurt," I called.

When he didn't respond, I ran after him and tried to kick him back. Unfortunately, and typically, my toe caught the carpet and I succeeded only in causing myself to stumble. I fell into him to break my fall.

"Back off," he snarled.

"What's the matter with you?" I whined.

"Bug off." He slipped into his bedroom and shut the door in my face.

"You bug off," I yelled.

Later on there was a knock at my door. "Janie?" Luke called.

"Whaddayou want?"

"Can I come in?" It's a good thing I wasn't going to say no, because he was already halfway through the door before he finished his sentence.

I glared at him.

"Sorry about before." He sat on Carmella's bed.

"Kicking me was an unprovoked attack," I said, my voice hard. I wasn't ready to forgive him just yet. "I didn't do anything."

He looked at his hands. "She dumped me," he murmured.

"Who?" I asked stupidly.

He looked at me like I was clueless. "Cassidy, who do you think?"

"Why?"

"Who knows? She had a bunch of reasons but none of them made any sense. Basically, she met someone else, but she says things weren't right between us before that. She claims that she tried to tell me but I didn't listen. Which is bull. I always listened to her."

"I never did like her," I said, raging inside at Cassidy's nerve. How dare she treat my half brother that way! The very idea of it angered me. But the hurtful thing was this: I had grown to like her, had shared my secrets with her, told her my weaknesses, so I felt personally betrayed.

"Well, I liked her," Luke said. "A lot. I still do. That's why I'm so pissed. She dumped me for a guy she met at a costume party. How could she dump me for some fool who wore an Oscar the Grouch costume stuffed with real garbage to make it authentic? It's so degrading. And he's not even great looking, unless you go for those guys who're built like freight trains."

"She's a loser. Forget about her."

"It's not that easy, Jane."

"Then get back at her. That's what I'd do. I'll even help you come up with a plan."

"You don't understand at all," he said, and left the room.

Carmella slammed the door, breathless. "Wait till you hear this."

I closed my Bubba folder and shoved it beneath my pillow. "What?"

"It's about Sharp and Chord."

"Oh brother. What about Sharp and Chord?" In spite of my disdain for Harmony and Carmella's appetite for ferreting out people's secrets, I was curious.

"Wait for Harmony. She's on her way over."

"You two must be the biggest gossips in the entire fourth grade," I said.

"Observing is not gossiping," my sister answered. She picked up her newest Barbie and began grooming her hair.

"Wanna borrow my markers? She could use a tattoo," I suggested, and received only a glare in response. I paged through a magazine until Harmony came skipping down the hallway.

"In here," called Carmella.

"My brothers are so stupid." Harmony said. She sighed, throwing herself on the bed next to Carmella. "You won't believe what they did this time."

"You really won't," added Carmella.

I waited patiently, aware that they didn't need any urging.

"They were *gambling* with their friends." Harmony waited for me to react. I didn't.

"We saw them." Carmella raised her eyebrow, coming close to achieving a Mrs. Perkins.

"With money," added Harmony. I wondered if either of those two girls could tell a story without the other.

"Real money," Carmella whispered, as if the FBI was monitoring the conversation. "We aren't going to tell Peggy and Elliot, though."

"I'm sure Sharp and Chord are relieved to know that," I drawled sleepily.

"But what should we do? We saw a TV movie where a man gambled away his brother's fortune and got murdered because of it," Carmella went on, acting like the future of the galaxy depended upon her and Harmony.

"Watch less TV. A sure remedy for the overactive imagination. Now go away. I seriously doubt Sharp and Chord are headed for disaster over a backyard card game."

"What do you know?" asked Carmella. "You're the most unobservant person in the neighborhood. I bet you don't even know about Tag."

"Tag?"

"Jason Blackshire's dog."

Stupidly, I took the bait. "What about his dog?"

Harmony frowned. "He died. Jason's really upset. . . . I think he even cried. His eyes looked red."

"Mr. Blackshire says it was old age, but we suspect poison."

"Poison?" I asked.

"Antifreeze," admitted Carmella. "There was a container of it in Mrs. Thomson's garage. She never did like that dog."

"Geez, your snoop-a-meters are working overtime today, aren't they?" I asked.

"We simply notice things, that's all," Harmony said.

"Go away," I moaned, covering my ears with my hands. I just couldn't take any more.

I raged at what Cassidy did to Luke. And in some crazy way, I felt responsible. I shouldn't have let her weasel her neo-hippie self into our lives. Maybe if I'd stuck with my original opinion of her, Luke would've seen through her and avoided all that heartbreak.

I decided to take action. I rummaged through my closet and found the cardboard carton of sewing stuff Aunt Jane had given me. I pieced fabric scraps together and embroidered. I sewed on buttons and beads. I cut yarn into strips. Then I used black acrylic paint to add the finishing touch. "Perfect," I said, admiring my work. "Who knew sewing could be this much fun?"

"Here," I said, tossing something onto Luke's bed.

He picked it up and examined it. "What the hell is this?" he asked.

"What does it look like?"

"Um . . . Barbie's evil twin?"

"Funny, Luke. It's a voodoo doll."

"A what?"

I sighed with exaggerated exasperation. "A voodoo doll. Geez, don't you know anything?"

"I guess not. What do I need with a voodoo doll?"

"Get back at Cassidy. Ruin her life."

"Ruin her life?"

"Remember that hairbrush she left in the bathroom? I

pulled the loose hairs from it and stuffed them inside the doll. That's how the magic knows who to curse." I threw my tomato-shaped pin cushion to him. "Stick it to her."

He caught it and laughed.

"Do it, Luke. It's easy. You've got the pins."

Luke looked puzzled. He held the doll before his face. "It does look kind of like her," he said. It didn't really. It was shaped like a gingerbread man and, courtesy of Aunt Jane's embroidery pamphlet, sewn with blanket and feather stitching and embellished with randomly placed beads. Two big red buttons were the eyes. The wild hair was made of strands of colorful frayed yarn. A black heart was painted on the left side of the chest.

"What do I do with it?" he asked cautiously.

"Make her suffer profusely."

"Why?"

"She's making you suffer," I answered pragmatically.

"Yeah. But Jane, I don't want to hurt her."

What a sap he was! "Oh, come on, Luke. Make her pay." I snatched a straight pin and stabbed it into the hole in one of the button eyes. A tremor of satisfaction coursed through me. "Some pain is just what you needed, isn't it, little lady?" Then I flashed Luke a big smile.

"You're insane," he said, laughing. He took a pin a poked it into the other eye.

"Put more feeling into it," I said, as if I was an acting coach. "And tell her what a loser she is."

"I'm never going to forgive myself if Cassidy has a seeing-eye dog next time I run into her," said Luke.

"We should be so lucky. . . . Just jab her again," I encouraged.

"Yeah, okay." He stuck a pin right through her black heart. "Guess you can't feel pain there, 'cause you're heartless, aren't you Cassidy?"

"Ow! That hurts. Stop it. Please stop," I squeaked, pretending to be Cassidy.

"What? You want more?" Luke asked the doll, and he drove a needle through her neck.

"Oh, the pain! Have mercy! Please," I cried.

"Beg, harlot, beg," said Luke, and he poked her again.

By the time Voodoo Cassidy had been appropriately pierced and punctured, Luke was laughing more than he had in days. So I guess my homemade voodoo worked, at least a little.

Self-motivation

"Have you heard the news?" Zander stood in front of me, smiling smugly.

"What?"

"I don't have to go to school next year."

"Right."

"It's true. Ask Mom and Dad."

"Squab, they aren't going to let you quit school after fifth grade. No way. They want us to go to college, remember?"

"Go ask. You'll see."

So I brought up the subject at the dinner table, intending to burst Zander's dream bubble in front of everyone. Imagine my outraged shock when Dad said, "That's true. Zander won't be attending Kingston next year, so you don't have to worry about him embarrassing you on the bus."

"You can't let him quit school. It's against the law!" I protested.

"We're radicals, Jane!" said Dad dryly.

"Then let me quit, too."

"We're not *that* radical."

Mom, ever the voice of reason, spoke. "Zander'll be homeschooled. Elliot's going to teach him along with Sharp and Jazz. Chord will be at Jefferson High next year."

"You're mean he's not going to be homeschooled anymore?"

"Not for high school. Elliot says he's not geared to get the kids through chemistry, physics, and foreign language classes."

"And Chord wants to meet some new girls," added Carmella.

We all looked at her.

"That's what he told Sharp. Harmony and I heard him say it."

"Eavesdropping again," groaned Zander. Then he turned to me. "I'll think about you while I'm living the good life."

"It's not fair, Mom," I protested. "Is Zander going to sit around the deMichaels' all day watching TV and playing games?"

"There's more to it than that. Peggy and Elliot say it's been great for their kids."

"So Zander will be playing musical chairs in Elliot's backyard while I'm stuck in English and math class every day? No fair."

"They do lots of cool stuff," said Zander. "Like today. They went to the state forest and made plaster casts of animal footprints."

"Oh brother." I rolled my eyes.

"Now, Jane, Elliot's very competent. Zander will flourish in Elliot's learning environment."

"Then let me go to Elliot, too."

"Jane, you hated music lessons, and Elliot centers

much of his curriculum on music. Besides, you're not self-motivated like Zander. We believe you need more structure."

"Not that again. I'm structured to death."

Once more, I saw the wisdom of the "life isn't fair" philosophy Mom had shared with me when I was a mere infant.

"So, Dad," I ventured. "What made you decide to run the marina and not go to work anymore?" It was early one Saturday and we were walking the piers to check on the boats moored in their slips.

He sat on the edge of the dock and adjusted his ball cap. "Jane, I *do* work. Or play, maybe. But I earn a living. I'm just lucky enough to love what I do. It wasn't like that at the insurance company."

"You hated it there?"

He removed his sunglasses. "Took me years to identify it, but yes, I did. I took that job before Luke was born, telling myself it was temporary until I found something else. And there I was, four kids and two wives later, still climbing the ladder, but the view got uglier and uglier. Faxes and conference calls and printouts. Clients and quotas and claims. But absolutely joyless. For me, that is. I'm sure some people there love what they do. But I was drowning without knowing it."

"So you quit because you wanted to work here?"

"Not really. I quit because I had to. For my survival. And once that was done, this opportunity came up. The timing was right. I'm happy here. Guess it was in my heart all along and I didn't know it."

"And now you do?"

"And now I do." He removed his hat and wiped away the sweat on his brow. "It was like this: . . . I'd lost my dreams, and by losing my dreams, I'd lost something else, too . . . some place in my soul. Life got soft and comfortable after my last couple of promotions, and it was easy to grow complacent. And that's what I did. Then one day I was training a young kid fresh out of college and I suddenly felt sick. Weak and exhausted. So I went looking for my dreams. It wasn't easy. I had to rummage around a bit. Strip away the outer layers to get to the core. But in the end, I found them. I found my dreams. And I think that makes me the luckiest man alive. Plenty of people never look for their dreams once they've lost them. Others never even realize their dreams have gone missing." He hugged me, kissing my cheek before letting go. "I'm a lucky man, that's for sure."

So later, I sat on the bank casting my line into the bayou, thinking about dreams. Where did they come from? Did they float around in the air like sound waves, waiting for someone to reach out and grab them?

Emma really knew her dreams. She talked about getting into a good college and then medical school. Fantasized about her future as a career woman successfully juggling family and work, or curing cancer or AIDS. Even spoke of retiring to one of the islands in the Caribbean.

My dreams were vague and blurry, like reflections on the water's surface. There were things I wanted to experience—seeing the world, falling in love, enjoying life, maybe finding fame and fortune. But those things were fluid and elusive, and I certainly never charted a plan to make them come true.

Goals

"We should set some goals for the upcoming school year," suggested Emma as she tore two sheets of paper from a notebook.

"Goals? Why?"

"It'll give us something to shoot for."

"I'll just refine my talents as a slacker." I yawned.

"No. You need to get over that and think of real goals." Emma uncapped her pen. "Hmmm . . ."

"I've got one." I grinned. "I'm going to get my first official kiss."

Emma laughed. "That's not what I meant, Jane. I was talking about stuff like 'make straight As' or 'run for class president.' "

"Oh. Boring stuff. I like my goal way better."

"But Jane, goals should be personal achievements."

"A kiss is definitely personal."

"But hardly an achievement."

"It's a matter of perspective," I explained.

Emma sighed and printed "JANE" in all caps at the top of one sheet of paper. Beneath, in smaller letters, she wrote "Eighth Grade Goals." Her script was tidy and precise. On the other sheet of paper she wrote "EMMA, Eighth Grade Goals." Then "Make straight As."

"Don't put that on my list. It'll never happen," I said.

"It could."

"Believe me, it won't." I grabbed the page labeled "JANE" and wrote "No Ds or Fs." My penmanship was barely legible. "This might happen. *Might*. It's at least within the realm of possibility."

"Really reaching for the stars, huh, Jane?" asked Emma.

"Just being realistic." "First kiss," I penned beneath "No Ds or Fs."

Emma snatched the pen. "Soccer team captain," she wrote on the EMMA page.

"Paint my yucky purple bedroom," I added to my list.

Emma sighed. "Jane, set some serious goals. Something that's a challenge."

"These are challenges. A kiss, passing grades, new paint."

"Kisses and paint are superficial."

"Then you don't know much about kisses," I retorted.

"Like you're an expert." She rolled her eyes and wrote "Learn to count in French, Russian, Mandarin, and Spanish" on her sheet.

"Boring. You really need to get a life," I said.

"I happen to like my life," she responded as she added "Raise money for Ronald McDonald House."

"How are you going to do that?"

"Collect soda can tabs. We can leave a jar in each classroom for kids to put tabs in. And advertise on the announcements. Make posters. You'll help, won't you?"

"I guess," I said and wrote "$ for McD's" at the bottom of my list.

She slid my page toward her. "Turn in every assignment," she printed in bold letters. "Now sign it." She handed me the paper.

"What?"

"Sign it."

"Like a contract?"

"Yeah. Like a contract. You'll never get into college if you don't act more responsibly."

For some insane reason, I scribbled my signature at the bottom of the page.

"I'm going to hold you to it," Emma said. "At least the homework and grades and money for Ronald McDonald House."

"Oh brother . . . sign yours, Miss Save the World."

Emma proudly wrote her name in cursive letters beneath her clearly stated goals. Her first, middle, and last names. And I knew she took her commitments seriously, because that was how she was. I inhaled and reread my goals. And I made a secret promise to myself that I'd follow through and prove to Emma that I wasn't a total loser.

I watched Carmella and Harmony playing in the backyard. They had layers of silky scarves draped over their bodies and flowers braided into their hair. They sang as they danced in a ring around the trunk of a towering pine tree. Then our dog, Banjo, bounded across the yard, and I laughed to see that he, too, was adorned with a wreath of flowers encircling his neck.

I envied the nine-year-olds the unselfconscious abandon of their games. They seemed so happy and innocent. I wondered whether, if Chord and Sharp had been girls, we'd have played the kinds of games Harmony and Carmella did.

"Hi, Carmella," I called as I walked outside to the deck.

She and Harmony shrieked and ran into the bushes. "It's a human!" they cried.

I sat on the steps. "What are you playing?"

"We're sea nymphs," explained Carmella, peeking out from behind an azalea. "A fisherman caught us in his net and took us to his hut. He believes we have the magic to grant him wealth and eternal life. We escaped, but we need to find our way back to the ocean. And we're terrified of human beings."

"Want to play?" asked Harmony.

"Yeah, play with us," said Carmella.

"No thanks. . . . Well . . . sure!"

"We'll get you dressed," said Harmony. By the time Harmony and Carmella had wrapped me in silks and woven flowers into my hair, Peggy was calling them in to get ready for their dance class. I sat on the steps, still in costume, with Banjo sleeping at my feet.

"Interesting outfit." I turned to see Chord standing at the fence. "Hey, guys, come here. You won't believe your eyes." Zander, Jazz, and Sharp appeared next to Chord.

I felt awfully silly but put on a good face. I stood up, bowed, and said, "I'm a sea nymph trapped on land and searching for the ocean. This is my sea horse." I gestured toward the sleeping dog.

"You're weird, Jane," said Chord.

"Actually, she's not. She's as normal as they come, which is what makes this weird!" said Zander, shaking his head. Why did I feel he'd insulted me by calling me normal? Wasn't normal good?

I scratched Banjo's neck to hide my embarrassment.

In second period on the first day of eighth grade, Emma slipped into the seat next to mine. "How's it going?"

"Okay. Chase was in my science class. He looks as good as ever. But we have assigned seats and I'm in the front row. He's in the back. He didn't even speak to me."

"And you're surprised? Jane, he's a snob." Emma opened her notebook and wrote the date neatly at the top of the page. Then she looked at me. "Don't forget about your goals. Did you write down all your assignments? I'm accepting no excuses."

I yanked my homework pad out of my backpack and slid it across my desk. "It's the second class of the first day. I have no assignments."

Glamour

Someone grabbed my arm as I scanned the school hallway looking for Emma. "Jane?"

I turned to see a tall girl whose hair was dyed so auburn it was nearly purple. I looked at her quizzically, saying nothing.

"Don't you remember me? Second grade?" she asked.

"Um . . . I barely remember second grade," I answered.

"I'm Jenny Danielson. Sat next to you. I'll never forget the time you taped a 'Kick me!' sign to Mrs. Perkins's back. She was furious. And you actually laughed. I though she was going to hit you."

I studied the girl standing before me. "Jenny Danielson?" She was striking, even if it was mostly paint and dye and hair gel. Her makeup made her cheekbones look like they'd been sculpted by Michangelo, and her brown eyes were lined and shadowed like Cleopatra's or those of some other exotic princess. Her hair was short and spiky and bold. "Didn't you move away midyear?" I asked after sifting through my elementary school memories.

"Yeah. West Coast. L.A. and then San Diego. We're back, though. My dad got transferred with his last promotion."

"You look so different," I said. "So stylish."

"You haven't change one bit. Even your hair is the same. I'd have recognized you anywhere."

Self-consciously, I ran my fingers through my hair. "Never really thought about it," I muttered.

"Jenny." Chase McClusky slipped his arm around Jenny's waist.

"See you around, Jane," she said as she breezed away with Chase in tow. A few steps later, they both turned to glance back. I heard Jenny giggling. I blushed and walked in the opposite direction, choosing to take the long way to science class.

> *Dear Bubba,*
> *Not another Barbie girl. Yuck! Even back in second grade Jenny Danielson acted like she was French pastry and I was moldy bread. And naturally, Chase McClusky is following her around like she's a dog in heat. Barf!*
>
> > *Still the same,*
> > *Gabriel*

I leafed through the photo album until I found my second-grade picture. My hair hung just past my shoulders, my freckles were scattered across my nose like pepper on a fried egg, my smile was just a little crooked. I stood in front of the mirror. Jenny was wrong. I *had* changed since second grade. My hair now fell down my back, and my adult teeth had filled in those gaping holes where my baby teeth had once been.

But I could be more stylish. Who couldn't? I taped a photograph from *Vogue* to the mirror. Now, that's chic, I thought, evaluating the model's sleek makeup and flirty haircut. With a pair of scissors in my hand, I snipped at my hair and combed through it with my fingers. I snipped again, glancing at the picture. I wanted to look like that girl from the magazine. She was glamorous and mysterious. I cut some hair away from my face and pushed it back. It fell forward again. I slapped some gel into it and spiked it up. It wilted. I cut some of the length from the back. Now one side was longer than the other, just like in the picture. It looked fabulous on the model, but I simply looked bedraggled. It just needed to be evened up a bit. I hacked away.

The floor was littered with hair. My hair! And when I looked in the mirror, that pitiful girl staring back at me looked like a newly-hatched baby bird. I sat on the edge of the bathtub and wept.

"Jane?" I heard my father's voice. I stuffed a washcloth into my mouth to muffle my sobs. "Janie? I'm coming in, okay?" The doorknob turned. "What happened?" he asked, astonished at my tearstained face and my tattered hair.

"Oh Daddy," I cried, and threw my arms around his neck.

He held me there for a long time, stroking my back. Then he quietly said, "Want to go to the hairdresser?"

"People will see me," I moaned.

"Hang on." He came back with a ball cap, which he placed on my head. "Let's go."

The hairdresser did the best she could to fix the mess I'd made, and my new do actually looked rather flirty. It wasn't what I'd had in mind, or what I truly wanted, but it was passable. I decided to fake it out. "It's just the look I was after," I announced at dinner, and Dad winked at me from across the table. He was truly my hero that day.

> Dear Bubba,
>   Remember when I asked you to hook me up with some visibility cream? Well, forget that. I don't need it anymore. Send vanishing cream instead. I really need to disappear.
>
>   Insincerely,
>   Harriet Hairdresser
>   (Alias Gabriel)

Sharp and Jazz were standing on the porch when I opened the door. "Hi, Jane," said Sharp. He was looking quizzically at my hair but had the grace not to comment.

I wish I could say the same thing for Jazz.

"What happened to you?" he asked.

"Nothing."

"Where'd your hair go?"

I resisted the urge to touch my head and chose not to respond. Instead, I smiled at Sharp. "How's everything?"

"Why'd you cut your hair?" Jazz persisted. "It's wild. Really wild."

"Shut up, Jazz," said Sharp. "Did Zander tell you that Peggy's taking us to the courthouse Friday so we can see how the legal system works? Chord's ditching his classes to go with us. Peggy said you can come, too, if it's okay with your parents."

Anything was better than a boring day at school, even joining the homeschool brigade. "Mom's at the grocery store. I'll let you know when she gets home."

Jazz was still looking at me wide-eyed. "You look way different," he said. "Way different."

"Unfortunately for you, you look the same as always," I snarled, and then I slammed the door.

"Peggy *needs* me to go to court with them Friday," I told Mom, running my fingers through my very short hair. "Course, that means I'll have to miss school," I added in an offhand manner.

"Oh, how tragic!" said Mom. "We all know how you hate to miss school."

"Can I go?"

"You'll have to make up your assignments."

"No problem," I replied, aware that the odds of that happening were remote.

Decorum

Dad told me to wear a dress. "Appropriate attire for the courtroom," he explained.

The boys all wore shirts and ties. "I didn't even know you owned a tie," I said to Sharp in the deMichaels' crowded van on the way to the courthouse.

He laughed. "I do now."

"Don't I look great?" asked Chord, posing theatrically.

"You don't want us to answer that," said Jazz, "because you look like a buzzard."

"With that haircut, Jane looks more like a buzzard," said Chord.

"As if you know anything about fashion," I retorted. The boys all laughed, and I found myself wishing for that vanishing cream again.

"They don't have hair like that in any fashion magazine I've ever seen," Chord said.

"Since when do you read fashion mags?" asked Jazz.

"He keeps *Cosmo* under his mattress," said Sharp.

"No, I don't," Chord protested. "But obviously, Jane doesn't either."

Peggy turned from the front seat. "Enough, Chord."

"I was only kidding."

"Enough. You know better than to be so rude. Now, kids, there are some things we need to establish before we get there. First, who knows what courtroom decorum is?"

I should have kept my big mouth shut. "That's the way the place is decorated," I said brightly.

"You're as dumb as dirt," said Chord with a sneer.

"Chord, be a gentleman," chided Elliot as he changed lanes.

"Yeah, Chord, be a gentleman," mimicked Sharp, and the boys all laughed again.

Peggy cleared her throat. "Actually, courtroom decorum is the expected code of behavior. It applies to everyone—the lawyers, the witnesses, the defendant, even the spectators. That's what we'll be—spectators." Peggy proceeded to tell us what to do and what not to do. There were a lot of not-to-dos, especially for Zander and Jazz.

We watched two fairly short cases. In between, Peggy explained what was going on.

"Not exactly as exciting as *Law and Order*, is it?" Chord said sarcastically.

"But this is real life. The futures of real people are at stake here," said Peggy gravely. "That man who robbed the convenience store will go to a real prison and leave behind his real family. They have real bills to pay and a real father to miss."

"Yeah, well, he was *real* stupid to commit armed robbery," said Chord.

"Or real desperate. Not that that makes it right, but

have some compassion, son. All of us do regrettable things at times. Some are merely more costly than others."

"Yeah, well, that's not what you'd be saying if I was the fool who'd held up a convenience store," Chord countered.

During the next break I thought about what Peggy had said about the cost of regrettable choices. It made sense to me. I sure had a long list of things I wished I could take back, and my pitiful haircut wasn't even at the top.

When we were little, Chord liked to tease Sharp and me by saying we were going to get married and have a bunch of dumb but musical children. "Dumb like Jane, musical like Sharp." All the others would laugh, but it made Sharp and me angry. Sharp would run after Chord. I'd side with Sharp, eager to preserve my reputation. Sharp, always fast, usually tackled Chord quickly. "I don't love her," he'd shout as he punched his brother in the ribs or stomach.

I'd join Sharp in defending our honor. "I'm not dumb," I would scream, kicking Chord.

"Sharp and Jane, sitting in a tree . . . ," Chord would laugh as he fought to escape.

"Take it back," Sharp would insist.

"K-I-S-S-I-N-G," Chord would chant.

Then the whole thing would fizzle out without anyone coming to serious harm.

One day, though, when Chord started taunting us, Sharp didn't play by the rules. Instead of protesting and launching an attack, he grabbed me and planted a kiss on my cheek.

"Yuck!" I cried, wiping my face with my shirt.

"Gross," said Jazz while Zander, Harmony, and Carmella giggled.

But it was Chord's reaction that was priceless. "You kissed her!" he accused Sharp, looking at his brother as if he'd bitten the head from a cockroach.

"Yeah. What about it?" Sharp smiled big.

"That's disgusting!" Chord shook his head in disbelief.

"Don't you ever, ever do that again," I said to Sharp, shoving him in the chest. I rubbed my cheek with my hand. I just couldn't get rid of that kiss that was stuck to my face.

Later, blushing, Sharp apologized. "Peggy suggested it. She said something like that might shut Chord up. You just have to act like it's not bothering you."

And Peggy's wisdom paid off, because Chord quit teasing us after that. But I still didn't trust Sharp when he got too close to me.

A Kiss Is Just a Kiss

"We've done great on our goals," said Emma toward the end of eighth grade. We were making our weekly rounds collecting can tabs. "I just wish I hadn't gotten that B-plus in math last grading period."

"Yeah, a B-plus in math really sucks, doesn't it," I replied acidly. I'd been at least as surprised as my parents about my report card. All As and Bs, except for the C I got in PE because I refused to dress out every day. "Geez, Emma, it's amazing what happens when you actually turn in your assignments."

"That's what I've been telling you since we met, Jane."

"That was the best report card I've ever gotten. I hope my parents don't do something stupid like raise their expectations. No sense encouraging them."

Emma sighed. "Don't you want to do well? For yourself?"

"Never gave it much thought," I replied glibly, dumping a jar of tabs into a plastic bag.

"You're as smart as anyone else. Just lazier than an old

hound. If you channeled your energy you could do amazing things."

"Being a slacker is a practiced art, Emma. Something I doubt you'll ever achieve."

"Let's hope not." Emma poured the final jar of tabs into the bag. "This project was a great idea. I'm glad we planned to do it."

"You planned, Emma, and drafted me. You deserve the credit."

"Teamwork," she said, slapping me a high five that knocked the bag from my hands. The tabs spilled and scattered everywhere.

"Way to go," I said as I swept up a handful of aluminum.

"I think we've had a great year."

"It's been pretty good. I'm ready to get out of middle school. It's so juvenile."

Emma laughed like she always did when I made ludicrous, superior-sounding remarks. "Right, your maturity puts you way ahead of the rest of us."

"Don't I know it."

"You should be proud of yourself, Jane. You've done great on your goals."

"But I didn't meet all of them."

"Which ones?"

"The kiss and the purple room. I can't go to high school unkissed with a bedroom that thinks it's a plum."

"You're worried about *those* goals?"

"My 'superficial' ones, remember?"

"How could I forget? So paint your room, and as for the kiss, it'll come when the time is right."

"It's on my list," I said, tossing my head and walking away as the bell echoed through the hall. "I'm determined. See what your influence has done to me?"

"Guess what?" Mom asked in an excited tone. I was in a rotten mood. I had only two more weeks of middle school and *still* hadn't kissed a boy. Not only was that one of my goals, committed to with my signature, but according to Jenny Danielson, the lack of that kiss also made me a loser. Apparently she had eavesdropped on a very private conversation between Emma and me in the locker room after PE, and Jenny wasn't the sort to let even the tiniest fragment of gossip go to waste. She said I better head straight for the geek table in the lunchroom when I got to high school. And she said it in front of my entire English class. Most of the kids laughed, but a few sank in their seats. I guess they were afraid they'd be Jenny's next victims.

I went back at her with a remark about how she'd kissed every available candidate and then some, so she'd have to sit at the slut table, but somehow my remark didn't have the same impact as hers.

"Jane?"

"What, Mother?"

"Watch your tone of voice, young lady. What's got you in such a foul mood?"

"Nothing," I snarled. I knew that if I told her what had happened, she'd fill the room with useless platitudes I'd heard a gazillion times already.

"Well then, cheer up. I've got some exciting news for

you. Aunt Jane is coming into town for the graduations—yours and Luke's."

"What?" I tossed my head, rolled my eyes, and groaned.

"I'm putting her in your room. You and Carmella can sleep in the family room."

"You're giving Aunt Jane my room? And letting her come to my graduation? Mom, how could you?"

"You should be flattered. Aunt Jane wouldn't do this for just anyone, you know. She seldom travels anymore. It's only because you're her favorite niece—"

"Lucky me."

"You are lucky. Honestly, Jane, I don't know what's wrong with you. Luke, Zander, and Carmella adore Aunt Jane. Everyone does."

"Mom, it's bad enough that the squabs are coming to graduation. It'll be the most embarrassing thing in the world having Aunt Jane there. She'll probably wear some ragamuffin dress she got at a rummage sale. My friends will never let me live it down. People don't forget things like that, you know."

"If that's truly how your friends think, they aren't worth a moment's notice. And your aunt has excellent taste. She's just not terribly interested in those superficial things. And God bless her for that!" Sometimes I wondered if Emma was Mom's spiritual daughter—they thought so much alike it scared me.

"Easy for you to say. My life sucks." As I stormed to my room, I heard my mother berating me for my behavior.

Every competent slacker knows how to get just what she wants.

"Mom, I really think this purple room will be too much for Aunt Jane."

"Do you?"

"It's awfully bright, and her eyes are sensitive. I remember Dad telling us that when he sent her those rhinestone studded sunglasses last summer."

My mother gave me a look that translated to *I've got your number*. "Your concern is touching. You're worried about Aunt Jane's eyes?" she asked mockingly.

"Exactly. Maybe a nice yellow or blue would be right. What do you think?"

"I think you regret this hideous purple you insisted on years ago!"

Mom, Carmella, and I went to the paint store, where we examined all the little paint chips and compared one tint to another. The colors had poetic names like Summer Wheat, Ice Castle, River Moss, and Strawberry Sundae. Carmella wanted a pink called First Love that would have been perfect for cupcake frosting and made me want to puke. "No way," I said. "Pink is out."

"You got to pick the purple," Carmella replied, crossing her arms and stomping her foot.

"Compromise, girls," Mom urged. "Or the purple stays."

We finally agreed on a blue called Skydancer that reminded me of a Siamese cat's eyes. It took four coats of paint to cover the purple. Dad didn't trust me with a paintbrush (another benefit of being a successful slacker), so he and Mom spent the weekend redoing my bedroom.

By the time Aunt Jane arrived, we had fresh paint and new comforters. I agreed to wait until after Aunt Jane's visit to tack my Godzilla posters back on the walls.

I dropped my bicycle next to the marina's main building. My father was standing on the patio talking to some boaters. I wandered off in search of Luke, who was replacing a stretch of worn-out planks on one of the piers. "Hi."

He looked up. "You would show up right when I'm driving the final nail."

"I've always had impeccable timing," I responded. "Besides, you oughta be glad to see me. I brought food."

Luke dropped the hammer into the toolbox. "That changes everything."

I unzipped my backpack and handed him a sandwich. "Got a little smashed. Sorry."

"Still edible," he said. "But I've gotta go wash my hands."

We walked to the workshop. "So Luke, how do you get a guy to kiss you?" I asked.

He slid the toolbox onto the shelf and brushed off his hands. Then he looked hard at me. "What boy?" he asked.

"Any boy."

"You'd let just any boy kiss you?"

"Well, there's one in particular I like, but he barely knows my name."

"You mean Chase?"

"How'd you know?" I asked, astonished.

"I connected the dots. You talk about him all the time."

"I do?" I hadn't realized I'd been that obvious.

"Yeah, you do. He sounds like a jerk." He went to the sink and turned on the water.

"Well, he's not. Unfortunately, he's not likely to kiss me. He's got a girlfriend. But there are plenty of other guys. What do I do?"

Luke laughed as he rinsed the soap from his hands.

"This isn't funny. It's serious," I snapped.

"Sorry. I'm not trying to offend you. Look, Jane, if you asked me how to flush out an outboard or tie a clove hitch, I could easily help you. But kissing . . ." Luke looked uncomfortable. "It's . . . um, well, there aren't really any rules or guidelines that I know about. Kisses just happen."

"So if you feel like kissing someone, what do you do?"

The workshop wasn't very well lit, but I sure thought Luke blushed. "I don't know. It depends on the situation . . . the chemistry."

"You're not much help."

"Sorry. But things like kisses . . . I'm not certain there are any straight answers." He dried his hands. "I'm starving. Let's go eat."

"Hurry up, children. We don't want to be late. Aunt Jane's plane lands in an hour, and you know how that airport traffic is," Dad called down the hall. I'd already lost the argument that maybe I should stay home just in case Aunt Jane, who had a two-hour layover in Houston, called to announce a change of plans. (Wishful thinking.)

"Maybe she'll get hijacked," I snarled.

"Enough, Jane," said Mom. "Zander, go wash your face and change your shirt. Hurry."

"Why doesn't Luke have to come?" I asked, miffed at the injustice.

"Wish I could. I'm on my way to work, birdbrain." He thumped me on the nose.

So we piled into the car and drove to the airport, where Carmella managed to con Dad into buying her an over-priced stuffed frog in the gift shop while we waited for the plane to land. Aunt Jane came strolling through the terminal dressed like an exotic bird in a Pepto-Bismol-colored jumpsuit trimmed with flamingo pink feathers. Her hair, which had been an orange puffball the last time I saw her, was now silver blond.

"She's fabulous," sighed Zander.

"She's magical," sang Carmella.

"She's insane," I said. "Like Big Bird on steroids."

I felt a slap on my shoulder. "Behave yourself," warned Dad.

"Jane," called my mother, not to me, but to the flamingo woman. Arms outstretched, she rushed toward the security station plastered with Do Not Enter signs. Zander and Carmella followed her, and shortly thereafter I witnessed the spectacle of them all hugging. I even saw a couple of pink feathers wafting through the sterile airport atmosphere. Dad laughed and dragged me into the huddle. It was so humiliating that I was instantly blushing brightly enough to compete with Aunt Jane's outfit.

When we'd finally untangled ourselves and were heading for the baggage terminal, Aunt Jane took my hand and said, "Look at you, Sweet Jane! All grown up, and so lovely." She held my hand and pranced through the airport like she was the Queen of England.

Dad gave me the eye, so I pretended I had to adjust my shirt in order to extricate myself. Fourteen-year-olds don't hold hands with ancient wonders in public places. It's un-heard of!

"Come tell me about your life," said Aunt Jane, moving over on the love seat to accommodate another person (that person being me).

"There's nothing to tell," I replied, but the look on Mom's face told me to sit down and talk, so I did. I told Aunt Jane about my friends and my classes and the other usual stuff, and it sounded awfully dull, but she acted like I was Homer reciting *The Odyssey*. With such a rapt audience, I began to elaborate and embellish, and soon even Zander was laughing at my exaggerated version of middle school. Naturally, my stories centered on the ineptness of the teachers and the intelligence, glamour, and daring superiority of the kids.

"These modern children are certainly a smart bunch, aren't they?" Aunt Jane said to Mom. But I thought I saw her wink, and wondered if all kids throughout history had thought themselves a cut above the previous generations.

When I marched through the auditorium at graduation, I scanned the crowd for my family, my heart thumping and my fingers crossed. I could just picture Aunt Jane, dressed like some exotic bird or beast, sitting in the front row and blowing an airhorn when they called my name. Then I saw her perched between Dad and Carmella, wearing a sedate navy blue suit and a string of pearls, looking as respectable as the first lady at the presidential inauguration ceremony. Relief flooded through me, and I gave Zander a thumbs-up as I paraded past, eyeballing other families with their eccentric members.

By the time Aunt Jane left, I'd grown attached to her. Mom was right, she was great: entertaining and adventurous and funny. And she understood me and the issues in my life even though she was a relic. "Aunt Jane's totally cool," I said on the way home from the airport. Mom groaned and Dad laughed.

"I kissed Bryan Latham," I whispered to Emma in the backseat as Dad drove us home following a graduation party at Madison's house.

"Bryan Latham?"

"Yes."

"But he's such a creep. Why him?"

"My goals. Remember? Besides, I couldn't go to high school unkissed."

"Jane, that is the dumbest thing I've ever heard. I could go a lifetime without being kissed unless the right guy came along. Bryan Latham? Yuck. How was it?"

"Awful. He tried to put his tongue in my mouth but I clamped my teeth shut. He slobbered! It was so gross."

"Yech! I wouldn't even want him to touch me. I mean, he's not bad looking, but he's such a creep, and you know he's going to tell everyone."

"He better. That's the whole reason I did it."

"Jane! That's disgusting."

"At least I won't have to sit at the geek table."

"Don't you get it? You wouldn't have had to anyway."

"Insurance."

"Would you do it again?"

"No way."

"There's hope for you yet."

Chord sat beside me on the steps. "So, Jane, did you meet your eighth-grade goals?"

"What?"

"Your eighth-grade goals. You know, no Ds or Fs, paint your bedroom, collect can tabs, all that."

"Oh, that. How'd you know about that?" I asked.

"Harmony and Carmella."

"Figures. Those little snitches."

"So did you?"

"Actually, yes," I said proudly.

"Even the kiss?" he asked.

I felt the blood rush to my face. "They told you about *that*?"

"Wasn't it on the list?"

"Maybe."

"So did you get your kiss?"

"Maybe."

Sharp walked up. "What's goin' on?"

"I'm just asking Jane about her eighth-grade goals," Chord said, grinning.

"Oh yeah, her goals. How'd that work out?" asked Sharp.

"He knows about it, too?" I asked.

"Everyone knows," said Chord.

"Everyone? Who's everyone?"

"Use your imagination," Chord replied.

"So did you meet your goals?" Sharp asked.

"None of your business."

"What about the kiss? Did you kiss anyone?" he persisted.

"I have the right to remain silent. . . ." I crossed my arms in mock defiance. Both boys laughed.

"You don't have to tell us, because Carmella already did," said Chord, smirking.

"What?"

"Does the name Bryan Latham ring a bell?" Chord taunted.

"Bryan Latham? Carmella was making that up," I protested.

Sharp shook his head. "I don't think so. Not with the way you're blushing."

"I'm not blushing. It's just way too hot out here."

I heard them laughing as I jumped up and stalked into the house.

"Carmella!" I shouted when I shut the door. I wanted to wring her neck.

> Dear Bubba,
>   Remember that time I requested vanishing cream? I'm renewing that request. There's nothing I want more than to vanish. Immediately.
>   And Bubba, why'd I have to get the loudmouth of the millennium as a little sister? And why'd you tell her about Bryan Latham? You must've, because I certainly didn't. Can't anyone around here keep a secret?
>
>   Exposed,
>   Gabriel

Moving On

"I've got the cushiest new job in the world," said Luke one hot August afternoon.

"You quit working for Dad?" I asked, astonished. Luke loved the marina at least as much as my father, maybe more. He introduced efficient ways of performing tasks and suggested upgrades on a regular basis. Dad and Uncle Grayson always praised his accomplishments. I couldn't imagine him working anywhere else.

"No, I'll still be doing that. But Mr. Marcello hired me to live on his houseboat. Can you believe it? I'll be getting financial rewards for not living at home anymore."

"What's wrong with living here?"

"Nothing, really. But this is the opportunity of a lifetime."

"What about when Mr. Marcello wants to use the boat?"

"He won't. His company transferred him to Singapore for at least the next three years, so I'm his caretaker."

"Won't you miss us?" I asked, dismayed at the idea of his leaving. He was still my hero.

"It's not like I'm the one going to Singapore. I'll be a few miles away."

"Dad's okay about it?"

"Yeah. Geez, Jane, I'm not a five-year-old. I'm a high school graduate with a job. And this is a business agreement between me and Mr. Marcello. It has nothing to do with Dad."

I'd been shocked when Luke announced that he didn't want to go to college and Dad backed him up. We'd been fed from the college spoon since infancy, so it seemed the natural follow-up to high school. Then, at the dinner table one night his senior year, Luke said he wasn't going. I held my breath, expecting my parents to lose it. Instead, Dad simply asked him why not, and Luke explained his position, which was basically that he'd never liked school and wanted a full-time job at the marina. He enjoyed working on boats and being around the water. All Dad said was, "I just hope your decision is based on your dreams and your vision of the future and nothing else, son."

"It is," Luke assured him.

"Fine, then. And if you ever change your mind, that's fine, too."

I've always admired, but also envied, the relationship my father and Luke share. They seldom fight, and seem to understand one another without speaking.

I briefly enjoyed the delusion that once Luke moved out I'd have my own room. The truth slapped me like a bucket of icy water. "I can finally move the computer out of the dining room," Mom said.

"It's fine in there," I protested.

"Jane, we need an office. Dad does most of the marina paperwork at home, and it's inconvenient for him to have his files scattered all over the house. This is the obvious solution."

"Not to someone stuck in a room with Carmella."

"Forget it. Now help me move these file boxes, Jane."

When Chord went to Jefferson High after his three years in the homeschool brigade, I assumed Sharp would return to real school, too. That he'd start wearing normal clothes and behave more like Chase McClusky and his crowd. I should have saved myself the trouble.

One afternoon the last week of summer vacation, Sharp and Jazz were sitting on my front steps waiting for Zander to get home from a dentist's appointment so they could go to the park and play basketball.

"Where've you been?" Jazz asked when I walked up to the house.

"The marina. I was helping Luke paint the bait shed."

"That explains your tattoo," said Sharp. "Looks like a duck."

I studied the blob of paint on my forearm. "A goose, actually," I corrected him. "Where'd you get that shirt?"

He was wearing a red T-shirt with Stonegate School of the Arts silk-screened across the front in black letters. "Had freshman orientation today," he said. "You like?"

"You're going there?"

"Yeah."

"Since when?"

"Got accepted last spring. I told you about it, remember?"

"I thought you meant you were enrolled in their summer program. You're not going to Jefferson with Chord and me?"

"Chord's transferring to Stonegate. Elliot's got lots of friends who teach there. He says it's a great school."

Stonegate is a magnet school offering classes in music, visual art, drama, dance, and writing. It made sense for the deMichael boys to go there—they would fit right into the curriculum and the student body, an eclectic group of avant-garde kids, freaks, and misfits who listened to underground music and NPR, read the *Village Voice* and the *Onion*, wrote their own zines, and bought their clothing at thrift stores, garage sales, and flea markets.

I sat beside Sharp on the steps. "You know, you'll have a lot of social adjustments to make. You've been out of commission for three years."

"You still don't get it, do you, Jane?" Sharp looked at me and folded his arms across his chest. "I was home-schooled, not dead. I still saw people, did things. Maybe you're the one who needs more exposure. . . . Did you ever think of that?"

I was stunned. Me? Lacking exposure? I was at least as savvy as any of the homeschool brigade. "What do *you* know?" I headed for the house, and while I didn't exactly slam the door, I did shut it with more force than necessary.

Priorities

It was the third week of high school, which wasn't significantly different from middle school, except the kids were older, the student body was larger, and the social scene was even more rigid. Luckily, Emma and I had computer technology and PE together, and Madison was in four of my classes.

"So Jenny Danielson's still playing the same old games," Madison said as we claimed a table (I wasn't able to identify the "geek table" I had worried so much about) in the lunchroom.

"Yeah. Just with a new supporting cast. Wonder what happened to Chase?" Samantha asked.

"He's going to Harmon Academy," I told them.

"Looks like Jane's going to have to find a new superman," teased Madison.

"Oh please," I said, "don't remind me of those days. That whole thing was so middle school."

Emma just laughed and shook her head.

Carmella and Harmony came into my room and sat on the bed. My mattress sank beneath their weight. Now that they were almost twelve, I suddenly realized they took up a lot more room than they used to. "Want to know a secret?" asked Carmella.

"No," I said.

"It's a juicy one," Harmony told me.

"I don't want to hear your secrets. Or more accurately, someone else's."

"You'll want to hear this. It's about Chord."

I wondered what Chord could have done that was so enticing and scandalous. Curiosity got the better of me. "What about him?"

"We heard him telling Sharp all about it," said Carmella.

"They didn't know we were there," added Harmony.

"He's going out with a girl from his school."

"Her name is Ashley, and she has big—"

"Boobs," whispered Carmella. They both giggled at that as if it was risqué.

Harmony broke in. "And a nice butt. And she's in the theater track, which means—"

"She likes drama."

"You got all the dirt, didn't you?" I asked.

"There's more. Chord wants Sharp to go out with Ashley's friend."

"Named Meagan."

"But Sharp isn't sure if he wants to. He says she's too pushy. We'll update you when we know more."

"You two little spies really need a new hobby," I said, reaching for my math book. "Have you considered stamp collecting? Quilting? Drowning each other?"

"You just wish you knew everything we know. Like about the Blackshires," said Carmella.

"The Blackshires?"

"They got a new dog," added Harmony.

"A golden retriever puppy."

"Named Kenneth."

"Jason walks him all the time."

"And Mrs. Thomson claims that it barks all night long."

"Jason walks Kenneth by her house on purpose just to rile her."

"Enough, already," I cried, sticking my fingers into my ears. "Scram."

"Can I make dinner tonight, Mom? I'm supposed to cook a lot, according to my nutrition teacher. It's my homework. You'll have to sign my menu so she'll know I actually did it."

"If Jane's cooking, I'm going to Waffle House," said Zander.

"If it's Jane's homework, then Jane cooks," said my mother.

"I'm eating next door," called Carmella.

"Very funny," I said.

I followed the recipe Ms. Parker had handed out. We didn't have any Swiss cheese, so I substituted cheddar. And I used garlic in place of onions because of Carmella's allergy. Later I realized I forgot to add the basil but put the pepper in twice.

"Mom, how will I know if I get food poisoning?" Zander asked, slipping into his seat.

"You'll know," said Carmella. "You'll turn green. And your stomach will lurch."

"She doesn't know anything. You won't turn green," I said. "But this dinner is going to be good and you won't get food poisoning,"

"How far is it to the hospital, Mom? Just in case? Can you get me there in time?"

"Enough, Zander," said Dad. "Looks delicious, Janie." He sounded like he had reservations.

"Smells safe," admitted Carmella tentatively.

"I can't believe you people!" I exclaimed.

"Hey, this is good," said Zander in shock after taking a bite.

"What did you expect?" I asked, but I was relieved that he was eating and couldn't answer.

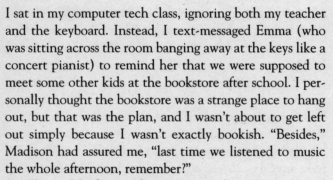

I sat in my computer tech class, ignoring both my teacher and the keyboard. Instead, I text-messaged Emma (who was sitting across the room banging away at the keys like a concert pianist) to remind her that we were supposed to meet some other kids at the bookstore after school. I personally thought the bookstore was a strange place to hang out, but that was the plan, and I wasn't about to get left out simply because I wasn't exactly bookish. "Besides," Madison had assured me, "last time we listened to music the whole afternoon, remember?"

"Emma," I whispered, trying to get her attention, and signaled her to check her messages. She glared at me and kept working. Sometimes Emma exasperated me. For over three years I had tried, without success, to influence her with my slacker mentality. She didn't comprehend how much easier life could be without such an overblown work ethic.

I met her at the door when the bell rang. "Why'd you ignore me?"

"I was working. Doing the assignment, which I know you didn't do."

"I did part of it."

"You're not even a *real* slacker," she said, hitting me at the core of my being.

"What?"

"You do expend energy—tons of it—on stuff. You just pick useless things like text-messaging me about the same thing six"—she checked her cell—"make that *seven* times in one day. A real slacker wouldn't bother repeating herself."

I felt like I'd been slapped. All these years I'd carefully cultivated an image that she was now calling a sham. I gaped at her, unsure how to respond.

She grinned. "You know I'm right."

Was she?

"See you after school. Bye, Jane." She walked away, and I knew she'd won that round.

Dear Bubba,

What does an overachiever like Emma know about the basic tenets of slackerism? Nothing, that's what. Emma's my best friend and I'm grateful to have her in my life, but sometimes I wish she'd loosen up and live a little. I mean, what kind of person would stay home and study for a biology test when she could be at the movies with Madison,

Samantha, and me? That's just not normal behavior. She needs to learn to prioritize.

Complacently,
Gabriel

The Entrepreneur

"Janie," my father said when he sat down.

"Yeah, Dad?" I clicked the remote, changing the channel to *Iron Chef*, my current favorite show.

"You interested in making some cash?"

"Doing what?" I hoped it was nothing too strenuous. As a slacker (I still claimed that title, in spite of Emma's declaration), I am a firm believer in energy conservation, especially when it comes to *my* energy.

Dad crossed his arms. "At least give me the courtesy of turning off the TV and looking at me."

I reluctantly punched the Power button. The secret ingredient on this episode was grouper, which our freezer was packed with after my father and Uncle Grayson's last fishing trip on the *Annika Elise*. "What's up, Dad?"

"There's a tournament at the marina on the twenty-second. Thought I had everything covered, but apparently there was a communication breakdown. Mr. Castle, who usually brings in his trailer, is already committed to the swap meet at the fairgrounds. I'm not sure I can get someone else on such late notice."

"So what do you want me to do?" I asked.

"Grill hot dogs, hamburgers. Maybe sell drinks and chips. Nothing fancy."

"And you'd pay me? How much?" It was one of those Einstein $E=mc^2$ deals. Income − (output + energy spent) = net gains or losses. For me to commit, the gains had to be significant and risk free.

"I'll buy the products. You cook them and sell them. Pay me back what I fronted and you keep the rest. Although you'll probably need help, so you'll have to split it with your partner. I thought Zander could join you."

"Zander?" That was something I hadn't written in to the equation. Another drain on energy expenditure—a huge one.

"It's a big event. You could make some decent money."

"Yeah, maybe. What if we don't sell enough to cover your expenses? We get nothing?"

"We'll work it out. Calculate a fair wage based on what you do sell. But we've hosted this tournament for years, so I doubt that will be an issue."

"If Zander'll help, I'll do it," I agreed with some reluctance. "Emma's got a soccer meet in Orlando that weekend anyhow."

Sharp was loading Elliot's van with some equipment. "What are you doing?" I asked.

"Elliot and I are going out to Sage Creek. He wants to record the wind in the saw grass and the water flowing over the stones. Stuff like that."

"You still do that?"

"Yeah."

"Doesn't it get boring?"

"No. It's pretty exciting, actually."

"It's kind of weird, you know. Regular people don't do stuff like that."

"So what do regular people do?"

"I don't know . . . watch TV, eat, work, sleep. The usual."

"Well, *that* sounds pretty boring to me." He shoved the last box of tangled wires into the back of the van and shut the doors. "See you later."

"Zander, I told you to chop the onions. We're almost out."

"I will when I finish this, Jane. Don't be so bossy."

I flipped the burgers on the grill. "You're lucky I let you in on this deal. Dad asked me, you know."

Zander capped the jar of pickle relish and set the cutting board on the table. "I don't see why I always get stuck chopping the onions."

"Quit your whining," I snapped. My demeanor changed completely as a man approached. "Yes, sir, how can I help you?" I smiled like a model in a toothpaste ad.

"Two cheeseburgers," he said.

When he paid me, I held his change over the tip jar on the table just long enough for him to get the message. "Score!" I said, nudging Zander as the man disappeared into the crowd. "I'm good at this."

"*We're* good at this," he corrected me, wiping away the tears streaming from his eyes. "And you're doing the onions next time."

. . .

"You smell like a barbeque grill," said Carmella, wrinkling her nose.

"Go away. I'm taking a shower after we count our profits," I said, raking a handful of quarters across the table. "Okay, Zander, we still owe Dad another fourteen dollars and eighty-seven cents."

"You're paying him in all change?" asked Zander.

"Don't have enough change. We'll have to give him some of these ones."

"But he probably doesn't want all those loose coins."

"Money's money," I said, dumping Dad's share into a vinyl bank bag.

"So, Dad, when's the next tournament?" I asked when I handed him the front money. The bag was quite heavy because of all the change rattling around inside.

"We have one next month," he said. "The Elks Lodge is raising money for St. Jude's."

"Can Zander and I do the food again?"

"You think it was worth it?"

"Heck yeah. We each made two hundred twelve dollars. And eighteen cents."

"You should put some of that in the bank. And put some aside for supplies for the next tournament."

"You could front us again."

He laughed and held up the bulging bank bag. "I don't think so. I might need a dump truck to get this to the bank."

"Maybe I'll add potato salad to the menu next time," I said. "And brownies or cookies. I love to bake."

"Don't bite off more than you can chew," he warned.

"Me?" I asked in disbelief. "I'd never do that."

Dad didn't comment—he just grinned and started stacking quarters on the table.

Electricity

As tenth grade unfolded, I found myself so caught up with my friends, many of whom now had driver's licenses, that I hardly saw the deMichaels—not even Jazz and Harmony, who spent about half their time at our house. I distanced myself from my own family, too. I dashed home to change clothes, slept there, and shared the occasional meal with them, but my focus was elsewhere.

Sometimes, I felt an empty sort of loneliness—like my hours were filled but my essence wasn't. It was as if some crucial wire had been disconnected, so that even though other wires were snaking their way into my system, without that essential wire, the current wasn't as smooth as it should have been.

On those lonesome days, the end of the pier next to the *Annika Elise* became my cocoon. I'd dangle my legs over the side and watch the bayou meander past and the birds overhead swoop and soar. Almost by accident, I came to relish the sound of the water lapping on the banks and the cries of the birds. I found the rustle of the wind in the reeds comforting. Oddly, at those times I felt close to Elliot and Sharp, whose obsession with sound defined them.

I was with Emma and Madison at the music store when who should walk up but Chase McClusky. He still looked basically the same. He was wearing a navy blue blazer emblazoned with the coat of arms representing the private school he now attended. Sure, he was taller, and his face was more sculpted than it had been in eighth grade, but not radically so.

He approached us with a big smile and wrapped his arm around me like we'd been the best of friends. He had someone with him—a kid who reminded me of Bryan Latham. "Jane, we sure had some great times back in the day, didn't we?" Chase asked. The puzzled look on Emma's face told me she was just as surprised as I was.

"Hi, Chase," said Madison.

"Girl, you look fabulous," he said. "Love what you've done with your hair."

Madison blushed and feathered her bangs with her fingers. "Thanks."

"This is Dylan," he said, gesturing toward his friend. Then he swept his arm to include the three of us. "These beauties made middle school bearable. Emma, Jane, and . . . um . . . um . . ."

"Madison," said Emma, touching Madison's forearm.

"As in Madison Avenue," laughed Chase, but no one else did, not even his pal, who seemed confused.

I looked at Chase like he was a space alien. Suddenly,

the hero-worship I had channeled his way all through middle school evaporated. This guy, who I'd built up to be some Adonis, was so impressed with himself he made me want to barf.

"Hey, Jane, didn't you have a fling with my man Bry somewhere along the line?"

"No. You must be thinking of someone else," I said.

"But Jane—" Madison began.

"Bryan was never my type," I interrupted. "He tried too hard to be you, Chase."

Emma's eyes got huge, and I saw her suppress a giggle. Madison simply looked lost, so I knew we'd have to explain it to her later.

I glanced at my watch. "We're late, ladies. Let's go."

I marched out of the store, leaving Emma and Madison with no option but to follow me. We all burst into laughter and exchanged high fives as we headed for my mother's car.

"What was wrong with me?" I asked as we were pulling out of the parking lot. "I actually thought he was fabulous! He's so pathetic."

"He's still cute—you have to give him that," said Madison.

"Till he opens his mouth," said Emma. "Too bad he doesn't come with a Mute button."

"You rock, Emma," I said, laughing.

"Yay! I love chili," said Carmella.

"Put that spoon away. This isn't for you. It's for the tournament this weekend. Not expensive to make, but I can sell it for three dollars a bowl. Add fifty cents for garlic bread. Twenty-five cents for grated cheddar. Another fifty for cole slaw. It's quite profitable. And it's less labor intensive than hamburgers and hot dogs because all the cooking is done in advance. A big pot of chili is a worthwhile undertaking."

"So let me have one bowl," she said.

"For three dollars."

"Oh, come on, Jane."

"Okay then, I'll give you the family discount. Two fifty."

"Just forget it." She tossed her head and snatched a pear from the fruit bowl. "And for your information," she added, "you spend so much time in the kitchen that you don't know anything that goes on around here."

"Excuse me? That's not your attitude when you're grabbing a fork and digging into one of my creations." I put the lid on the bubbling pot of chili. "Besides, *nothing* goes on around here."

"Yeah, what about Harmony and Zander?"

"Harmony and Zander?"

"She thinks he's cute."

"He probably doesn't even notice her."

"They played cards yesterday. Just the two of them."

"Oh brother. I guess that left you with Jazz, eh?"

"Actually, I've got my eyes on someone else."

"Who?" The process of elimination took only a moment, considering the two twelve-years-olds were still homeschooled.

"Jason Blackshire," she announced smugly.

"Jason Blackshire?"

"You know . . . at the corner. He's so nice, and he's funny, too."

"That skinny kid?"

"Lean, Jane, lean. Don't tell anyone. It's a secret."

"There's no such thing as a secret with you and Harmony around."

Renaissance Man

"I love baseball season," Emma said with a sigh. It was spring of tenth grade and we were sitting in the hot sun on the bleachers watching a scoreless baseball game.

"Since when?" I asked.

She grinned. "Since I started seeing Tony. When else?" Tony was an outfielder for the team. It had surprised me when Emma admitted to being attracted to him. I'd always imagined her hooking up with the chess club type, not a center fielder with an average IQ but fabulous shoulders. "He's throwing a party tomorrow night. Wanna go?"

"Sure, I guess."

So there I was at Tony's backyard bash, feeling awkward because the only person I knew well was Emma, and she was mostly occupied with Tony. I was talking to some kids when something hit my hand. "Yuck!" I cried as I dropped my drink, which splashed on my hand, jeans, and shoes.

I turned around to see an orange Frisbee rolling across the grass.

"Oops." A dark-haired guy was standing a few yards away looking embarrassed. His smile was illuminating. I'd seen him around school and knew he was a junior, but I'd never met him. He picked up the Frisbee, then said, "Sorry," rolling his *R*s with a lyricism that charmed me to my toes.

Tony laughed. "Raphael, you're such a klutz."

Raphael (who I came to call Demonseed as our relationship regressed) had straight white teeth and eyes like black coffee. "Not all of us were born to be ballerinas" was his reply. Everyone laughed. He grabbed some napkins from the table and wiped my dripping hand, an act I found oddly intimate but not offensive. Tony made introductions, and somehow, by the time Emma and I were piling into her car, Raphael was holding my hand and making plans to see me the following night.

My first evening with Demonseed was pretty standard. We went to a movie and for a bite to eat. But to me, it was anything but standard. I thought he was the handsomest, funniest, nicest guy on earth. And he liked me!

That night was the first time I'd been kissed since that awful graduation party where I allowed Bryan Latham to put his mouth on mine only because it was on my goal list. Raphael's kiss was nothing like Bryan's. This one sent sparks flying through me.

For our second outing, along with Emma and Tony, we met a bunch of other kids at the bowling alley. I didn't even have to be embarrassed about my pitiful bowling scores, because Rafael's were worse than mine. Tony kept calling him Gutter Ball. Emma kept saying I was distracting him. The whole evening was very entertaining and I couldn't wait to see Raphael again.

Our third time out, I affectionately called Demonseed Rafi. "Raphael," he said firmly. Turned out he was awfully vain about his name. "Raphael was one of the greatest artists of the Italian Renaissance."

"Raphael was also a Teenage Mutant Ninja Turtle—a hero on the half shell," I replied, remembering the endless childhood hours I'd spent at the deMichaels' watching their DVD collection of those sewer-dwelling turtles and fighting over who got to be which turtle when we played in their backyard. "And one of the archangels," I added in tribute to the celestial companion of my alter ego, Gabriel.

Demonseed laughed. "Either way, it's Raphael, not Rafi, understand?"

"Sure, I understand." I started humming the theme song to the *Teenage Mutant Ninja Turtles*. Raphael covered my mouth with his hand, then with his lips. Wow!

Dear Bubba,
  I'd rather be named after a Teenage Mutant Ninja Turtle/archangel in heaven/Renaissance artist than some fossilized aunt who drools in her soup. Can I change my name to Donatello?
              Cowabunga, dude!
              Gabriel

· 152 ·

"Jane made cookies," Zander said to the deMichael boys. "Her own special recipe." He grabbed the platter from the counter and took it into the family room.

"Careful you don't break your teeth if Jane made them," cautioned Chord.

"That'd be fangs, in your case," I snarled at him from the kitchen.

"I'll chance it," said Sharp. "Pass 'em here."

"Me too," said Jazz.

"Hey, Jane, although it pains me to admit it, these are great," called Chord

"You're getting crumbs everywhere. Geez, Chord, chew with your mouth closed," said Jazz. "Don't you have any home training?"

I walked into the room just in time to see the last cookie disappear. "Glad you guys held back," I said sarcastically.

"Make another batch," said Sharp.

"I'm going to have to. Those were actually for someone else."

So I returned to the kitchen, where I measured, mixed, beat, and baked another batch of cookies, which I carefully packed into a box for Raphael before the neighborhood gluttons struck again.

I slipped through the front door, wishing I could have stayed out even longer, but Mom and Dad were super strict about my curfew. On my way down the hall, I heard Harmony and Carmella giggling. "What's so funny?" I asked. Their giggles turned into hysteria. "Carmella?" I grabbed her arm. "Were you and Harmony spying on me again?" Their facial expressions gave them away. "You . . . you brats!"

"You were kissing him," said Carmella.

"So what? You were watching—that's the psycho thing. Geez, you two are twelve years old. When are you going to outgrow this annoying behavior?" I stomped away, resisting the urge to strangle those two sneaky little spies.

The Little Neighbor Boys

"I could sure use a couple more hours' sleep," I muttered to myself when the alarm buzzed the first day of eleventh grade. I hit the Snooze button and turned over.

"Hey, Jane. Wake up," said Zander brightly.

I glanced at him standing in my doorway already fully dressed. "You look good." I yawned.

"Thanks. I woke up early. First-day jitters, I guess."

"It's weird we won't be going to the same high school," I said.

"It'll be weird going to school at all," replied Zander. "But I think I'll like Stonegate. Sharp says it's great, as school goes, anyhow."

"I'm going to take a shower," I said sleepily.

Dad poured himself a second cup of coffee. "Do you need a ride to school, Jane? I'm taking Zander and the deMichaels to Stonegate on my way to the marina."

"No thanks, Dad. Raphael's picking me up."

"Well then, have a good day, sweetheart. Zander, have you seen my keys?"

The deMichael boys, dressed in their usual eclectic style, were waiting for Dad and Zander in the driveway when Demonseed drove up. Chord wore a red Dickies jumpsuit and flip-flops. Sharp had on a white dress shirt (untucked), a thin black tie, red and black board shorts, and soccer slides. Jazz was dressed in all black, as if he thought he was Johnny Cash. His hair was slicked to his head in a way I'd never seen before. I looked at them quizzically. "Does your school even have a dress code?" I asked.

"Sorta," said Chord.

"A loose one," added Sharp.

"Not strictly enforced," Chord said.

"Apparently not," I muttered as Raphael pulled away. "Bye, guys," I called out the window.

"So was that the boyfriend we've heard so much about?" asked Chord that afternoon.

"Who?" I asked.

"The guy whose car you crawled into this morning."

"Yeah, that's Raphael."

"The one you bake cookies for?" asked Sharp.

"Actually, yes."

"Why don't you go make *us* some cookies?" asked Chord. "Like now."

"Yeah. I'm starved," said Jazz.

"No cookies today. I'm making lasagna."

"Awesome!" said Zander. "Jane makes great lasagna." When I took foods and nutrition in ninth grade and learned to cook, I became Zander's hero. Considering his appetite, that was no surprise, but I liked it that he always praised my culinary skills, especially since there weren't many other things he'd ever openly admired about me.

"What time do we eat?" Sharp asked, laughing.

On a whim, I said, "Six o'clock. See you then."

"Really?" asked Chord.

"Sure," I said.

"I was never one to turn down a free meal," said Sharp.

"And me? Can I come?" asked Jazz.

"Of course. All of you."

"We'll be there," promised Chord.

"*Who* came to dinner?" Raphael asked me later on the phone.

"My neighbors. Sharp and Chord and Jazz."

"Why'd you invite them?"

"No reason. I said I was making lasagna and they wanted to come."

"A bunch of guys?"

"Raphael, are you jealous?" I asked incredulously.

"Maybe."

"That's really dumb. They're just my neighbors. I've known them . . . like . . . forever. You saw them this morning when you picked me up."

"Those freaks? You invited *them* to dinner?"

"They aren't freaks, Rafi."

"Raphael, Jane. It's Raphael." He rolled the *R* in his name every time he said it. I wished there was an *R* in my name so he could make it sound like a song.

· · ·

After the lasagna dinner, the dynamic between the deMichael boys and me changed again. Some of the awkwardness that had seeped into our relationships melted away and was replaced with casual friendliness. We didn't go out together, or even hang out at home very often (we all had friends and activities outside the neighborhood), but at least when we met in the yard or joined their family for a cookout, we could engage in conversation without a lot of negative energy between us.

Reflecting on the changes we'd gone through over the years, I realized what a brat I'd been, always placing myself in a position of superiority. I wondered if they knew it was my insecurity, and not really them at all, that had brought on such haughty behavior. They were so creative, quick, and confident, and I was Jane White, as generic as a yellow number two pencil.

Even Jazz, who'd been on the receiving end of more scorn than the others simply because he was with Zander so often, eased up around me. He actually joined me one night when he dropped by looking for Zander, who was out. "Whatcha doing?" he asked when he saw me sitting on the porch.

"Just killing time with George, Abraham, Alexander, and Andrew."

"Who?" He looked around.

I fanned a stack of bills. I pulled out a one, a five, a ten, and a twenty and pointed to the faces on the bills. "George, Abraham, Alexander, and Andrew. My favorite men, if you exclude Ulysses and Benjamin. They're on fifties and hundreds, but not terribly available."

"Where'd you get all that cash?"

"We worked at a tournament today. Sloppy Joes and barbeque sandwiches. Sides of potato salad and my barbeque beans, which are always a sellout. Made a bundle."

"Let me work next time."

"If we need you. Minimal labor costs mean a greater profit margin."

"But more hands means shorter hours, so it could balance out."

"I dunno. I'm pretty greedy."

"So I've heard. Anyway, if you need me . . ."

"Wanna watch a movie?"

"What movie?"

"I dunno. We can raid Zander's DVD collection."

"Great plan."

Steamrolled

I went about my life thinking I had the world on a string. The occasional fishing tournament, paired with my father's generosity, kept me in acceptable financial shape. Not that I had endless resources, but I managed to get basically what I needed. My social life revolved most tightly around Raphael and Emma, but a larger group filled the empty spaces. Mom normally let me use her car when I wanted. Things unfolded with relative ease.

Then, a few weeks into eleventh grade, my blissful, brainless complacency was shattered. I'd never dreamed that a ditzy blonde transferring to our school from one across town would be the source of my heartbreak, but from the first time I saw her I knew Trina was trouble. She walked into chemistry class, tossed her silky hair, handed Mr. Stanton a yellow slip of paper, and struck a pose. "She can share my table," David Horton announced.

"She can share my chair," chimed in Rusty Hayes.

"She can share my lap," called out Sammy Anders, and the guys all laughed. There was only one vacant stool in the chemistry lab—the one right next to Raphael. And naturally (life isn't fair, remember?), that was the seat Mr. Stanton assigned to Trina.

I smiled at Demonseed from across the room, but he was totally engrossed in Trina-gawking and didn't acknowledge me. I knew even then . . . Well, let's just say I had a premonition.

Trina whispered something to Raphael as she took her seat. He giggled. Giggled! It was disgusting and I wanted to puke. The next time I glanced their way, they were sharing a textbook in the coziest manner imaginable, Trina's blond head practically resting against Demonseed's thick brown hair. I knew trouble was a-brewing.

After class, I met Raphael at the door. "Walk me to French."

"Can't. I'm gonna show Trina around," he said, rolling the *R* in her name.

"Trina?" I asked stupidly, considering the fact that she was standing right next to him and I knew exactly who he was talking about.

"Trina, this is Jane. Jane, Trina," he said in an offhand way, almost as if I was a vague acquaintance. Then, to Trina, "I'll show you where the lunchroom is." And they were gone. He hadn't kissed me or even touched me.

I stood there alone—fuming, insulted, and . . . well . . . threatened. I followed the stream of kids going in the opposite direction.

I ran into Emma in the hallway. "Who was that blonde with Raphael?" she asked.

"New girl. Trina." I tried to roll the *R*, but failed, probably because I spoke through clenched teeth.

"Why's he with her?"

"Don't ask me," I snapped.

"Sorry," she replied, offended.

I stalked off toward my class, using a few of the choice French words my teacher had put on the forbidden list.

"I know we've been seeing each other for a while, and I really like you, Jane, but I never said we'd be exclusive."

I just sat there. Why make it easy for him?

"You're a great girl. We can still hang out."

Silence from me.

"Are you listening?"

"Sorry, Rafi. Did you say something?"

"Jane, this is important."

"I know. If you botch your SATs, you'll have to retake them."

"What? Jane, I'm not talking about SATs."

"Oh. I thought you were."

"Please listen."

"Raphael, don't you think we should see other people? I've been feeling restless . . . smothered. . . . Oops, I'm late for class. See ya." I blew him a casual kiss and dashed off down the hall.

Dear Bubba,

I hate it when you make me act like that. It was totally graceless, and pathetic, too. Stay out of my business and go destroy your own hapless relationships.

Scornfully yours,
Gabriel

P.S. Ignore those smeared words on the paper. They were not caused by tears. It must be raining.

Demonseed and I had been going out for six and a half months by the time the beautiful Trina Nobles transferred to our school. She had a golden tan and bright blond hair. Well, long-legged Trina set her sights on Raphael and he was powerless to resist. So it was adios, Jane, hola, Trina. Maybe he wanted a girl with a more exciting name than Jane. One whose name had an *R* he could roll. Who knows?

And what about all those sappy lines he'd fed me? "Oh Jane, my life was dull and meaningless without you." "You're the most beautiful girl I've ever seen." "I never want to be with anyone else." "You make my life complete." Barf. What crummy book or movie had he snatched those old standbys from? And was I really *that* gullible? Because I had fallen for them completely.

Part of what bothered me was that I felt like a stereotype. I couldn't eat, couldn't sleep. I was moody and irrational. My heart turned somersaults every time the phone rang. I desperately wanted it to be Raphael, yet was petrified that it might be. So there I was, a living, breathing cliché you might find in any cheap tearjerker romance on the shelves at the bookstore.

The worst thing was this: I had to sit through chemistry class every day while Rafi and Trina drooled at each other through Mr. Stanton's boring lectures about ions, electrons, and the periodic table. Trina wore short skirts and stretched her legs between lab stations during class.

She even dangled her strappy little sandal from her big toe, with its carefully polished flame-colored nail. Believe me, for Trina, chemistry had nothing to do with that stuff in the textbook.

> Dear Bubba,
>
> Why don't you send Trina (roll the R̲s when you read this) back where she came from? Her hair can't naturally be that blond. And her grammar is pathetic. Doesn't she know that double negatives cancel each other out? Enroll her in a remedial English class.
>
> Ain't got no shame,
> Gabriel

Voodoo Revisited

Luke was at the house when I got home from school one day shortly after Demonseed's defection. He was wearing his Ferrier's Point Marina shirt and a pair of dirty jeans.

"Just got off work," he said. "I'm starved." He pulled a container out of the refrigerator, opened it to peek inside, then replaced it. "How you doing, short one?"

"Don't call me that," I snapped.

"Touchy, touchy. So, how's the hero?"

"What hero?" I asked.

"Raphael, who else?"

"He ditched me. And for a brainless blonde."

"His loss, Janie. His loss."

"Then why do I feel so bad?"

"I dunno. That's part of the process," he said. "It gets better. And he wasn't all that, anyhow."

I felt an irrational urge to defend Raphael but said nothing.

. . .

A few days later, Luke drove me to the marina. "I've got something for you."

"What is it?"

"A surprise. It's in the workshop."

"What? An old Evinrude? A corroded swim ladder? A warped oar?" I asked, imagining all the junk typically strewn around the workshop.

"Nothing that fabulous. Come on." We walked across the grounds to a blue building. "Ta-dah!" he sang as he swept a towel from the workbench. Beneath it lay a weatherworn plank—probably a piece of someone's pier washed away in a storm. It was a jagged one-by-eight about two and a half feet long. On it Luke had painted a boxy figure that filled the entire board. "I can't sew worth a flip," he said.

"Sew?" I asked.

"Yeah. It's a voodoo doll for you. Like you made back when Cassidy dumped me." I looked at the plank. The figure was wild looking, but I realized immediately that it was supposed to be Raphael. It had bloodshot eyes, teeth like Godzilla, and hair made from crow feathers. A Teenage Mutant Ninja Turtle logo cut from a comic book was glued to the forearm like a tattoo. To top it off, Raphael's fishing license (which he'd left at the marina) was stapled-gunned across the figure's chest. "I couldn't find any of his hair," Luke explained, alluding to the hair I'd stuffed into the Cassidy voodoo doll. "I figured the fishing license was just as good. Hell, it's got his name and signature on it." He handed me a hammer. A big twenty-ounce hammer. A practical hammer. A tool to get the job done. He pushed a box of assorted nails across the workbench. "Ammo. . . . Well, Janie, let him have it."

"My pleasure."

I practiced voodoo on that plank with the fervor of a zealot until I ran out of ammunition. Then I hugged Luke. "Thanks, bro. That was great. Next time, let's use rusty nails."

"Sure. And barbed wire."

"Perfect. I could have had a successful career in the torture chambers of the Spanish Inquisition," I said proudly.

I took my mutilated and abused Raphael voodoo plank home, where I ensconced him in a place of honor with the punked-out Barbie dolls and my collection of plastic Gothosaurs.

Waffled

My father was doing the monthly financial reports for the marina. "Dad, I need some money. I'm going to the movies with Emma."

He glanced away from the computer screen and scribbled some numbers on a sheet of paper. "What ever happened to 'please,' Jane?"

"Please, Daddy." I used my syrupy sweet voice.

"Where's your fishing tournament money?"

"Spent it."

"All of it?"

"Yeah. Back-to-school stuff. My new wardrobe was expensive, you know."

"You need to get a job," he said.

"*Job*? Um, Dad, that word isn't in my vocabulary," I replied playfully.

"I'm serious, Jane. Get a job."

"Why?"

"Why? Because I can't afford to support your spending habits, that's why."

"What about my schoolwork? It might suffer if I get a job. You wouldn't want me to fall behind in my studies, would you?"

He pressed a button on the calculator and compared the number there to a figure on his spreadsheet. I suddenly realized how pathetic my timing was—I'd broken one of the most basic rules of being a successful slacker: never ask for cash when your benefactor is worrying about exactly that. Dad glanced up at me. "I don't remember your studies ever being a high priority, Jane."

Zander, who had appeared in the doorway, laughed. "Only when she's studying your wallet, Dad."

My father grinned. "That's the truth."

"You stay out of it, Lysander." I gave him *the look*. He'd been on the receiving end of *the look* since the day he was born. It used to intimidate him just fine, but lately it had lost its effectiveness.

Zander flashed me a smile that was nearly a smirk. "She could get a job at Waffle House," he told Dad in an offhand voice. "They had a Help Wanted sign on the door last time I was there."

"Look, squab, I don't need an employment agency here," I spat.

"Or those fast-food places are always hiring."

"Bug off. I don't see *you* getting a job."

"I mow lawns and stuff, remember? And help out at the marina. Hardly anyone will hire a fourteen-year-old. Besides, I'm not always hitting Dad up for money."

"That's true," said my father. "He's usually got more

cash in his pocket than I have in mine. So they're hiring at Waffle House?" He looked at Zander, who nodded. "Janie, why not try it?"

So that's how I ended up with a glamorous job slinging hash at Waffle House. My uniform looked pathetic. Black pants, white double-knit polyester shirt with black pinstripes, black apron, and of course, my name tag, which I called my identity crisis prevention utensil. Quite the fashion statement. I smelled like grease and coffee grounds by the end of my shift, but payday was sure fun, and I was never one to complain about a pocketful of tips, either.

"You've sure been cooking a lot," said Carmella.

"I like to cook," I said absently, not adding that it gave me something to do other than sit around fuming over Demonseed and Trina.

"We're cooking at Elliot's this month. We're learning ratios and measurements and stuff like that."

"Cool," I said dully, still vaguely resentful that I'd spent three long, boring years at Kingston Middle School while both Zander and Carmella got to do the Elliot thing instead.

"We learned all about baking powder. It's made from an acid, a base, and a filler. Usually cream of tartar is the acid, baking soda is the base, and something like cornstarch is the filler. When you get the mixture wet, it produces carbon dioxide, which causes cakes and stuff to rise."

"You learned that from Elliot?" I asked, astonished. I sure hadn't learned anything like that at Kingston Middle or Jefferson High. Of course, that doesn't mean no one had taught it.

"Yeah. It's basic chemistry. Didn't you know it?"

"Um . . . actually, no."

"We made bread yesterday. Yeast works almost like baking powder. It feeds on sugar and produces carbon dioxide."

"You're a walking, talking science book," I muttered.

"We're making cookies tomorrow. Maybe we could use that recipe you made up. It's my favorite."

"The one I made for Raphael? You can have it. I don't ever want to bake those again." I snatched a three-by-five recipe card out of my file box and slid it across the counter. "Might taste even better if you add a dash of cyanide."

Demonseed and Trina were going to the homecoming dance. It wasn't exactly a surprise, but I still got angry when I heard. Especially since they were double-dating with Tony and Emma. "You're a traitor. This is war," I told Emma.

"Don't be angry. It's not like Trina and I are friends. The guys planned it. They are best friends, remember?"

"You're supposed to be *my* friend."

"I *am* your friend."

"You're Judas in a strapless gown and heels," I accused her.

"My dress isn't strapless. Hers is."

"Thanks for sharing that tidbit with me. You're a real friend, you know it?"

"Come on, Jane. It's not my fault she came here and disrupted things. And if you and Raphael were truly—"

"Don't go there, Emma."

She sighed. "Jane—"

"Look, you have fun. Okay? Dance the night away."

"You could go with someone else," she suggested tentatively.

"Forget it," I snarled.

"What are you going to do that night?"

"Maybe Zander will play checkers with me," I said sarcastically.

"This isn't my fault, you know. You're not being fair."

"Emma, life isn't fair. Get used to it."

Invitation

I never was one to roll over and play dead. "Forget staying here for a checker tournament with Zander on the night of the homecoming dance," I said to Carmella. "I'm going!"

"With who? Zander?"

"Zander?" I replied scornfully. "I'd never go to a school dance with my little brother. Social suicide. I might as well plaster *Major League Loser* across my forehead in big blue letters and call it a day!"

"Then who?"

"Sharp."

"Sharp?"

"Why not? No one from school knows him since he goes to that school for the arts. Won't that be great?"

"But he has a girlfriend. Some girl named Melissa. Harmony and I heard the boys talking about her."

"A minor inconvenience. A mere kink in the hose!"

"But Jane—"

"Keep this between us, Carmella, or you'll pay dearly."

"Aunt Jane's coming for the weekend. She'll be staying in your room," Mom said to me.

"Aunt Jane! Great. But those blue walls might be too sedate for her. Maybe we should consider some color that would get her blood pumping."

"Cute, Jane. The blue stays."

I winked. "I like the blue."

"Can you pick her up at the airport Friday? I've got an appointment I just can't squirm out of, and your dad's so busy rebuilding the finger piers at the marina that I hate to ask him."

"No problem, Mom."

It was great seeing Aunt Jane again. She was as feisty as ever, but she now wore a hearing aid and used a cane. Not just any cane. One whose handle was a carved vine, with the head of a lion at the top. The eyes were topaz stones, and the teeth quartz crystals. "If there was an alternative other than death, I sure wouldn't grow old," she said wistfully.

"You're not old, Aunt Jane," I said.

"Not of soul, Sweet Jane, but this body is another thing entirely." She didn't seem old to me. Her eyes sparkled and her laugh was strong.

We sat together on my bed and I updated her about my life.

I told her about Raphael. How he'd broken my heart, injured my pride, and shattered my trust. She completely understood. "Forget about him, Jane dear. He's not worth the trouble."

"But he's so fine—"

"And if he did it to you once, he'll do it again. Take it from me. I got burned once myself."

"You did?"

"Yes. And I gave him another chance and it happened again."

"It must have been awful," I said, trying to imagine Aunt Jane having a sweetheart who jilted her twice.

"It was, but I learned from it. Always find the lesson in whatever happens to you. That's what gives it value."

"What was your lesson?"

"That I was worth more than that. And never again did any man get the better of me. You're worth more, too, dear." She stood up and straightened her spine proudly. "We are Janes, after all." She tapped her cane twice on the floor for punctuation.

"Ugh! Emma, you can't even imagine how humiliating it was to sit there in chemistry while Trina babbled about the great shoes she bought for the homecoming dance. Like anyone cares what her shoes look like or how much they cost."

"She was telling you about her shoes?"

"No. She was talking to Lisa and Erin. But you better believe she made sure I heard."

"Couldn't have been on purpose, Jane. She's not like that."

"Are you taking up for her?"

"No, of course not. But—"

"Never mind, Emma. I keep forgetting you two are such great friends."

"Listen, Jane—"

"See ya. I'm late." I hurried away, stomped to my desk in French, sat down, and crossed my arms. During a review of verb conjugations, reason replaced some of my anger. I took my Bubba folder from my stack of books and binders.

> Dear Bubba,
>   Okay, I admit it. You're right. This isn't Emma's fault and I acted like a brat. I'll apologize to her at lunch. But don't think I'm going to take all this lying down. No way! Now I'm more determined than ever to show Trina and Raphael, and Emma, too, that I'm not a complete loser. See you at the dance.
>   Feeling shafted,
>   Gabriel

I crammed my latest communication with Bubba into the pocket of my folder. With a black Sharpie, I wrote "Letters to my Imaginary Enemy" in all capitals beneath "Bubba," which was written in green crayon in the wavering script of a second grader. Then I stuck my battered, tattered Bubba folder at the bottom of my stack of books and counted the ceiling tiles while I waited for the bell to ring.

"Hello, Sharp," I called. I was lucky to be coming home from the bus stop when someone was dropping him off at the curb. Now I wouldn't have to knock on the deMichaels' front door and ask for him. "Got a minute? I've been wanting to ask you something."

"Sure. What's up?" He met me at the property line.

"You just get home from school?" I asked, stalling as I tried to harness my courage. Now that I was face to face with him, this wasn't so easy.

"Yeah. Missed the bus 'cause I was talking to my music comp teacher, so my friend gave me a ride." He set an instrument case on the ground and placed a messy stack of music books on top. He looked slim and strong. And intimidating. How could Sharp look intimidating? And when had he gotten so tall? I was afraid I'd lose my resolve.

I had an armload of books and folders. I laid them on top of his sheet music. "What instrument is that?"

"Sax."

"You like it?"

"It's awesome."

"Um . . . how's school going?"

"Good enough." He looked puzzled, no doubt wondering why I'd called him over just to make small talk.

"Um, Sharp . . ."

Sharp folded his arms and stared into my eyes. "Is there something you wanted to ask me?"

"Yeah, actually, I was wondering . . . um . . . my school's homecoming dance is on the twenty-seventh, and . . . well . . . my date sort of fell through. So I thought maybe you'd want to go. With me." I felt my face flushing. I mean, Sharp and I took baths together when we were babies—this was weird!

"The twenty-seventh?"

"Yes. That's a Saturday. Two and a half weeks from now."

"Yeah. That'd be cool."

"You'll go?" I tried to hide my relief.

"Sure."

"Hope your girlfriend will be all right about it."

"Girlfriend?"

"Melissa?"

"Melissa? You mean Clarissa? She's Chord's girlfriend."

I wanted to kill Carmella, the queen of misinformation. Not only was she a major snoop, she wasn't even a very good one. Still, I was glad to hear Sharp wasn't entangled with some artistic girl from Stonegate. I didn't want to pull a Trina on some other unsuspecting soul. And Sharp, to whom I hadn't paid much attention in years, was looking at me with those Caribbean blue eyes and suddenly he wasn't just the little neighbor boy anymore.

A car pulled up and a kid of about eleven slipped out, lugging a guitar case. "Hi, Sharp," he called brightly as he slammed the door.

"Hello, Tyler," said Sharp. He turned back to me. "Gotta go. It's time for Tyler's lesson."

"Lesson?" I asked, picking up my schoolbooks and folders.

"I'm teaching beginning guitar." He shrugged. "Not a bad way to make some cash. . . . Let's go, Tyler. Bye, Jane. I'm looking forward to the dance."

"Chord keeps teasing Sharp about going out with you," Carmella informed me.

"Oh yeah?"

"He says Sharp's always had a thing for you."

"Really? What does Sharp say?"

"He just smiles and ignores Chord. Like always."

"What does he say about me?"

"Nothing. At least, not around me. He probably knows I'd tell you. He did ask about Raphael, though."

"What'd you tell him?"

"That he got another girlfriend and the two of you broke up."

"Why'd you tell him that?"

"Why not? It's the truth, isn't it?"

"He didn't need to know. What else did you tell?"

"That's all."

"Out with it, Carmella. I know there's more."

"Okay. I said Raphael was a creep. And Trina was a bimbo. And you wouldn't make those special cookies that we all like so much."

"You told him *that*?"

"Well, it's true."

"Don't say anything else. Just listen and report back." I couldn't believe I was enlisting Carmella (who should have been called Mata Hari) to spy for me.

"What are you wearing to the dance?" Carmella asked.

"I don't know. I've shopped around but nothing thrilled me. Everything's basically the same. I don't want to look like a paper doll of everyone else. I need to stand out so Raphael will take notice. I want to make him squirm." I threw myself onto my bed with more force than I intended. The headboard banged against the wall, causing three of my punkified Barbies to tumble from the shelf and jab me in the face with their plastic arms and legs. I tossed them aside impatiently. "Everything's so generic. I'm sick of being generic. I want to wear something out of character and unpredictable."

"Like what? A suit of armor?"

"Funny, Carmella. Real funny. I mean something girly and bold all at once. Something to make Raphael do a double-take and be consumed with regret."

Carmella spoke tentatively. "Jane, you keep talking about Raphael, but Sharp's your date."

"A technical glitch," I said. "Raphael's the target."

I picked up a Barbie whose white lace wedding gown was shorn off at the knees and held together in the back by a row of safety pins. A black leather belt with silver studs encircled her waist. The bodice was torn from neck to navel (except Barbie doesn't have a navel) to reveal a red lace teddy. Her hair was Sharpied and spiked. "Now, *she'd* get his attention," I said, holding her high.

"No doubt. And everyone else's, too," said Carmella.

"Carmella, you're a genius!" I exclaimed, jumping up. A puzzled expression crossed her face. "Mom, can I borrow your car?" I called down the hall as I grabbed my shoes.

Finding Things

Chord, Sharp, and a curly-haired girl slipped into the only empty booth. "Look what the cat dragged in," I said as they reached for menus.

"Nice outfit," said Chord, giving me a once-over.

"Smashingly stylish," added Sharp.

I pirouetted for them, displaying my official Waffle House attire of polyester perfection. "So what brings you to this gourmet dining establishment?"

"The service. Definitely the service," said Sharp.

"I thought it was the food," said Chord. "I heard the service here sucked."

"Ha. Ha. Ha," I said.

"This is Clarissa," Chord said. "Clarissa, my neighbor, Jane. She's Zander's sister."

"You know Zander?" I asked.

"From school," Clarissa said. "He's nice. And funny."

"He's okay, as brothers go."

"Hey, I'm a brother," said Sharp.

"And me," said Chord.

"Case closed," I said, winking at Clarissa. "Anyone ordering food?"

"We actually came to kidnap you. When do you get off?" asked Sharp.

"About an hour."

"We're having a scavenger hunt. Two teams. You and Sharp versus Clarissa and me," said Chord.

"A scavenger hunt?"

"You know what that is, right?" asked Sharp.

"Yes. You have a list and whoever finds everything first wins."

"Right."

"Elliot, as a neutral party, made lists," Chord told me. "So are you joining us?"

"She has to. She's my partner," said Sharp. "You will come, won't you?"

"Sure. Sounds like fun."

"Hey, Sharp, check your batteries," said Chord.

"Batteries?" I asked.

Sharp reached into his pocket and withdrew a small recorder. "In this scavenger hunt, we have to find sounds and record them."

"Huh?" He'd totally lost me.

"Here's the list." He handed me a sheet of paper.

I read the first five items aloud. "Howling dog, river flowing, siren, freight train whistle, squeaky wheel (extra point if it squeaks in B-flat) . . . I wouldn't know B-flat if it was whistling in my ear," I said.

"He would," said Clarissa, nodding toward Sharp.

"Might as well eat while we wait," said Chord, scanning the menu.

Spy vs. Spy

Chord, Sharp, and I were walking around the deMichaels' backyard discussing our scavenger hunt, which Sharp and I had won. "The crying baby almost defeated us," Sharp said. "Then Jane pinched a kid in a stroller and he squawked like mad."

"What? I did not pinch a baby," I protested. "Don't believe him, Chord."

"I don't. Even you wouldn't go that far, Jane."

"Actually, we got the crying baby at the grocery store. Along with the change jangling in a cash register and the automatic door." We heard a dull thump as Sharp's foot caught the edge of an upturned terra-cotta flowerpot nestled in a clump of monkey grass. It rolled across the path to expose a plastic pencil box, the kind kids use for their supplies in elementary school. Sharp picked it up. It held two items: a small spiral notebook like a homework pad, and a pen. He flipped open the notebook. Then he whistled one shrill note (it might have been B-flat) and grinned. "Interesting."

"What is it?" I asked curiously.

Sharp turned a page and began to laugh. "According to this, you kissed Raphael multiple times at eleven-thirty p.m. on September ninth. On your front porch. You were wearing a red tank top and a black mini-skirt."

"What?" I stood there stunned, processing what he'd said. "Give that here."

I tried to grab it, but he pulled it away and turned to Chord. "And on September twenty-seventh at nine-fifteen, you and Jazz had a fight. Apparently you sat on the papier-mâché model of the human heart he made for his science project."

Chord and I both tried to snatch the notebook, but Sharp spun away. "There's more. . . . On July seventeenth, Jane and Emma were discussing whose boyfriend was sexier. Jane said anyone named Raphael had to be sexier than someone called Tony."

"Let me see," I insisted, vaguely remembering the ludicrous conversation I'd had with Emma one boring summer afternoon. I grabbed at the notebook, but Sharp was quite a bit taller than me, and he held it over his head. "Get it, Chord," I called.

Chord reached for it, and the brothers were soon laughing and scuffling.

I moved in for the kill and snatched the notebook from Sharp's hand. I ran across the yard and hurriedly paged through it until I spotted Sharp's name. "August tenth. Ten-twenty p.m. Sharp was smoking something in the backyard. We aren't sure what it was." I fanned the pages until his name again caught my eye. "August twenty-first, nine-fifteen a.m. Sharp and Jazz used Elliot's special equipment to record a song they were working on. . . . September second, eight-twenty-two p.m., Sharp wore Chord's new green shirt when he went out. He didn't ask permission." By that time, both boys had converged on me and were making grabs for that revealing little pad of paper. I clasped it to my chest. "Wait!" I yelled. "We can all read it together. Or I'll read it to you—how about that?"

They agreed and we sat at the picnic table. I was sandwiched between the two of them. "Start at the beginning," said Chord. "Omit nothing."

So I did. I wanted to skip the bits about me, but they were both looking on, so I knew I couldn't get away with it. There were things recorded in the notebook that I'd already forgotten, like "August second, twelve-ten a.m., Jane broke her curfew but didn't get caught. Zander unlocked the door for her because she forgot her key." August eleventh must have been like winning the lottery for the two little snoops. They had recorded eight sightings that day—three about Jason, his dog, and Mrs. Thomson. The final entry in the juicy little tattler was from just the day before—it told about Sharp and Chord snitching a couple of beers from the deMichaels' refrigerator.

"Those little sneaks," Chord snarled when I closed the cover. His eyes were spitting fire. "I've had enough of Harmony and Carmella."

Sharp took the notebook from me. "Quite the little spy network," he said dryly, leafing through the pages and rereading the entries.

"I'll kill them." I clenched my fists. "Smash them like eggshells."

"Wait. Don't be hasty," said Sharp, returning the little book to its secret hideaway beneath the flowerpot. Then, with a mischievous smile, he devised a plan.

Overcooked

I looked around the marina's kitchen. Everything was in order, just as always. I knew if I ever left a mess, Dad would hire someone else to provide food for the tournaments, and this cooking-for-profit thing was one sweet deal. Great supplemental income to Waffle House. I'd sent Zander home to put away the leftovers while I'd taken care of the final few touches—wiped the counters, swept, cleaned out the sink. All that remained was the fryer, which I would tackle the next day, as the oil was still too hot to be handled. With a last satisfied glance, I clicked off the light, set the alarm, and locked the door. I strolled down the pier to Mr. Marcello's houseboat. The moon was full, blanketing the landscape in cool yellow luminescence. "Hi, Luke," I called. He sat on the boat's deck, fishing. I could hear music wafting through the cabin door. Everyone except the live-aboards had left just after dark, so we had the property mostly to ourselves.

He motioned me aboard. I sank into a deck chair. "Just call me moneybags," I said, patting the wad of bills in my pocket. "Not bad for a day's work. I made more in a few hours at that tournament than I make in two weeks at Waffle House."

"Those people gobbled up your fried fish, that's for sure," he said, casting his fishing rod into the water.

"So far the most successful menu item has been spaghetti. Inexpensive, tasty, and easy."

"Yeah. You really lost your shirt that time you did chicken dinners with baked potatoes and Caesar salads."

"Way too much overhead. And everyone wanted hot dogs. Who would choose that over a real meal?"

Luke lazily reeled in his lure. "You had this illusion of gourmet food served on fine china. These are fishermen, Jane. Beer-drinking, big-talking, hungry fishermen who get up at three a.m. to try to land a winner. They want to fill their bellies. Savoring a meal isn't their priority."

"At least I had the guts to try," I defended myself.

"Yep. Live and learn. Who's grilling out?" he asked, sniffing as he glanced up and down the docks.

"I dunno," I replied, not seeing anyone.

"I smell something. Not beef. Not seafood, either." He cast his rod out again. "So you're not going out tonight?"

"Rafi dumped me, remember?" I snapped.

"He's not the only person on the planet. You do have other options."

"Yeah right. . . . Hey, did I tell you I asked Sharp to the dance?"

"Sharp? You're kidding? Did he accept?"

"Yes. Thank goodness. Imagine how embarrassing it would have been if he'd said no."

"Sharp's smart. A nice kid. I like him."

"Yeah, he's cool. We've hung out a couple of times lately. Besides, imagine how Raphael's gonna react when he sees me with Sharp."

Luke leaned his rod against the cabin. "Jane, that's wrong. You can't . . . What's that I smell?"

I sniffed the air. The odor of smoke was strong.

"Oh my God!" Luke cried, jumping onto the dock. I turned to see him running toward the marina's main building.

Flames were licking through the windows at the sky.

I stood there. Speechless. Frozen. Scared to death.

"Call nine-one-one," Luke yelled. "And Dad. Call Dad." I grabbed his cell phone and punched in the numbers.

"Nine-one-one. What's your emergency?" said a detached voice.

My jaw wouldn't unhinge. It was like one of those dreams where you scream but no sound comes forth.

"Nine-one-one. What's your emergency?" the voice repeated.

"Fire," I finally squeaked. "A fire."

"What's your location?" asked the voice.

I wanted to kick someone. The building was aflame and that voice (I wasn't even sure if it was male or female) was so calm. I felt like screaming. Instead, I rapidly gave them our address. As I spoke, I could see Luke dragging things away from the deck near the building. Tables and umbrellas and chairs.

I called home.

"Hello?" said Carmella brightly.

"Get Dad," I barked.

"What?"

"Carmella, let me talk to Dad. Now."

She must have known I meant business, because I heard the phone clatter to the countertop.

It could only have been a matter of seconds but it felt like an eternity. Then I heard Dad say, "Jane, are you all right? What's going on?" The tone of his voice let me know that Carmella had prepared him for trouble.

Trouble? That's like calling diabetes a sugar rush. This needed a much more powerful word than *trouble*, but it eluded me then—it eludes me still.

"Fire. At the marina."

"Anyone hurt?"

"I don't think so."

"I'll be right there." The line went dead.

I stuffed the phone into my pocket and leapt from the houseboat. Then an explosion rattled the night. Flashes of red and gold splashed like fireworks. I couldn't see Luke. Couldn't hear anything over the ringing in my ears. Raced toward the burning building.

A sudden zone of thick, hot air hit me like a wall. My eyes teared. "Luke!" I yelled. But I got no answer. I looked about frantically. Everything was distorted. The building seemed massive, and the patio beside it lay skewed at a funny angle. The driveway seemed ridiculously narrow, and the parking lot tilted skyward. I shook my head. "Luke!" I shouted, making a megaphone of my hands.

Time and space didn't follow the rules. I remember fire trucks screaming onto the property with flashing lights. Coughing and choking on the smoke. My father talking to a man in a uniform. Uncle Grayson handing me a bottle of water. The ambulance. Thick black smoke. A light breeze crossing my face that momentarily displaced the breath of the fire on my cheeks. Someone from the fire department questioning me about the evening's activities. Zander and Carmella, with my mother, pulling me over to Mr. Marcello's houseboat. And fear, like a dagger, sinking deeper and deeper into my flesh.

"That was the stupidest thing I've ever done," Luke said. He sat on the edge of a hospital bed, fully dressed in jeans and a T-shirt. My eyes followed the path of scratches and scrapes and gooey scabs splattered up and down his arms. Noted the swelling of his left eye going black and purple.

"What do you mean? You didn't cause the fire, did you?"

"Course not. I don't know what made the building burn. I meant I was stupid to get hurt," he said. "I got too close. I wanted to save what I could. The Gallaways—the people with the twenty-seven-foot Hunter sailboat moored in that first slip—they'd been detailing their boat all day. They spread their sails and seat cushions out on the patio to dry. I was trying to salvage them when those propane tanks blew. Threw me all the way across the patio. At least it blasted me away from the blaze, eh?" he said with a grin.

"The building's a total loss."

"Dad told me. That sucks. He's playing it brave, but he's pretty slammed."

"I wonder what happened."

"I dunno. Electrical, maybe. Or some freak thing like a cigarette butt in the trash."

"Yeah, a cigarette in the trash. That must have been it," I agreed. "Are you okay? Does it hurt?"

"I'm fine. I'm not burned, just bashed around. I wanted to leave last night, but the nurse said I had to stay 'as a precaution.' " He sat up and squared his shoulders. "I'm out of here as soon as the doc releases me, which should be within the hour. And it won't be soon enough, believe me."

"Luke, honey."

I turned to see Sandy crossing the room. She looked pale.

"Mom. Hi."

"Morning, Sandy."

She gave me a quick squeeze and sat beside Luke, kissing his forehead. "You scared us last night," she said. Her thumb rested on his cheek.

"I'm fine, Mom. You know I'm not fragile."

"I know you're my child."

Luke looked at me and shook his head. "Geez, Mom, I'm twenty-one."

"You're still my child," she said.

I waved goodbye and slipped from the room, feeling they needed a private moment. Mom and Dad were at the nurses' station talking to a couple of people in scrubs. "Join Carmella and Zander in the lounge," said my mother. "We'll be done here in a minute."

Fire investigators sifted through the ashes. Uncle Grayson was engaged in a conversation with one of the boat owners. My father looked a little gray around the eyes and his smile seemed forced. He walked toward us, shifting the ball cap on his head and brushing his hands together. I stood with Mom, Zander, and Carmella next to Dad's truck. The charred skeleton of the building sprawled before us, black and ugly. That bonfire smell burned my nasal passages.

"The fire chief says it started in the kitchen," Dad said. "The oil in the fryer caught fire. Said it was cooked down to a tarlike consistency. Once it gets that hot, flames erupt and then—"

"The fryer?" I asked, my heart closing up and blood pounding in my ears.

"From the fish we cooked?" asked Zander.

"Yes. Could've been a lot worse. If one of the boats had gone . . . well . . . gasoline and fire are a dangerous combination. It would have spread quickly. We could've had a huge disaster." A curious look crossed his face. "It's amazing. The firefighters can accurately follow the path of the fire by examining the remains. You know what they told me? The filaments in light bulbs point toward the fire's source. Who'd have dreamed—"

"But I turned it off," I said, my voice firm but my heart pounding. "I turned the fryer off."

"Jane, accidents happen. No one's blaming you." He slipped his arm around me.

I twisted away from him. "But Dad, I turned it off," I insisted. "Zander, you were there. Didn't I turn it off? You saw me."

Zander shrugged. "I didn't notice. I was doing other stuff."

"Zander, you were standing right there."

He glanced away from me. "Sorry, Jane. I don't remember."

My mother intervened, eager to avoid an argument when everyone was already stressed out. "It doesn't matter. Carmella, you and Zander pass these water bottles out to the fire investigators. Let's go check on Luke, Jane." Luke was so stubborn that he'd refused to go home with us or Sandy and insisted instead on staying on the houseboat, which rankled both Sandy's and Mom's maternal instincts. My mother took my forearm and led me away. We walked down the dock toward Mr. Marcello's boat slip.

"Mom, I didn't do it."

"Jane, I saw the fryer. *Someone* left it on."

"Not me."

She sighed. "Jane, the evidence—"

"Then the evidence is wrong," I insisted.

My mother sighed again. She looked and sounded tired. "Everyone's safe. The building's insured. We didn't lose all our records since we set up that link to our home office. We can survive this. Just let it go."

When we got home from the marina, I kicked off my shoes and collapsed on my bed. I was physically and emotionally exhausted, and sick of the sympathetic (or drop the first syllable and go with pathetic—either one works) looks of concern my parents kept flashing my way. I yanked my folder off my desk and wrote furiously.

> Dear Bubba,
>   I turned that fryer off. I know I did.
> I'm careful about stuff like that.
> Firefighters can be wrong, can't they?
> Yes. I've seen movies where experts look

like fools on the witness stand. Experts
like firefighters. So why, you ruthless
enemy, are you letting me take the
blame? Have you no conscience at all?
Bet you're pleased with this latest
disastrous turn in my life. Smiling like
the cat that swallowed the canary? So
now, once again, I find myself wishing
for invisibility. Vanishing cream, please.

                              Smoked out,
                              Gabriel

Return to Sender

Talk about a strange twist of fate! Zander walked into the room as I was reaching for the remote. It was three days after the fire, and everyone was still on edge, though trying to disguise it. "You got a letter," he said, tossing an envelope at me while he leafed through the junk mail and bills. My curiosity was aroused, since I rarely got any mail other than all those college and "Join the Army" brochures every high school kid gets. I was doubly intrigued when I saw that there was no return address. Nor did I recognize the handwriting on the envelope. I held it up to the light, hoping to discover some clue about this mysterious communication. Nothing jumped out at me. It was simply a plain white envelope with my name and address scrawled across the front in blue ink. A postmark was smeared over the stamp.

I shrugged, ripped open the envelope, and extracted a single sheet of plain white paper, tri-folded. I shook the page open. Being an impetuous person, I didn't immediately read the letter. No. My eyes went straight to the closing. That was when my heart stopped. The name scribbled across the bottom of the page was "Bubba."

What does it mean when you receive mail from your imaginary enemy?

> Dear Gabriel,
>   I've taken your abuse for years. Don't you think you might occasionally write me a thank-you letter? Or perhaps send me a party invitation? A newspaper clipping, possibly concerning a certain fire? A postcard from some vacation paradise? Maybe a newsy missive updating me on your complicated life? Your constant whining, complaining, and blaming has worn me slap out.
>
>   Regrets,
>   Bubba

The telephone rang at least ten times before it was finally picked up.

"Hello?" A horribly shrill siren blasted my eardrum. Then it mercifully stopped and a voice said, "It's that doggone hearing aid. I do apologize."

"Aunt Jane?"

"I'm sorry. I can't hear you. Speak up."

"Aunt Jane?" I said louder.

"Yes, this is Jane," she said.

"Aunt Jane, it's me. Jane."

"Yes, this is Jane."

"No, Aunt Jane. It's me, your niece, Jane White."

"Who?"

"Jane White. Your grandniece."

"My favorite niece. Named for me! How are you, Sweet Jane?"

"I'm fine, thank you. I called to ask you something."

"You need to speak up, dear."

"Did you write me a letter? And sign it 'Bubba'?"

"A letter? Signed 'Mother'? No."

"Not Mother—Bubba, Aunt Jane. Bubba."

"I don't know any Bubba, dear."

I sighed. "Thanks, Aunt Jane. Bye."

"Be good, Jane."

"Yes, ma'am. Bye."

Oh well. It was worth a try.

Chord was waiting on the steps when I walked out the front door. "There you are," he said. "I've been thinking about you all day."

"Shh . . . do you want everyone to hear you? Come on."

I led him around the side of the house. It was there that he took me in his arms. "You smell so good," he said, nuzzling my neck.

"Not here, Chord. Not now. The window is open. Anyone could be inside watching. We need to be discreet."

"I'm trying, Jane, but you're so irresistible."

"Shhh. I'll meet you in our secret place. See you in fifteen minutes." I winked and left him standing there.

RSVP

I puzzled over the letter I had received from Bubba. It was impossible. . . . He couldn't have written to me—he was imaginary. Yet I held that precise impossibility in my hands. What was he doing communicating with me now, after all the other issues I was dealing with: Raphael's defection, Sharp's renewed presence as a significant player in my life, and the fire. The fire? Was Bubba like some phoenix born of fire? The thought chilled me. I took up my pen.

> Dear Bubba,
>   You're my enemy, remember? So the kinds of letters you're asking for are out of the question. Invitations and postcards and thank-you notes? Forget it. You don't send things like that to your enemy.
>
>   Don't call me, I'll call you,
>   Gabriel

I reviewed what I had written. No. I shook my head. That didn't work. I scratched through each line of text and tucked the note into my blue Bubba folder. Was I losing my mind? How do you answer a letter from an imaginary enemy?

Sharp saw me sitting on the porch and crossed the yard. "Hi, Jane. How's it goin'?"

"Okay," I answered dully.

"You still freaked out about the fire?"

"What makes you think I was freaked out?" I asked coldly.

"I dunno. Peggy said your mom told her you were having a hard time."

I rolled my eyes. "As if Carmella and Harmony aren't gossipy enough, now I've got my mother discussing me with the neighbors."

"I don't think it was like that. Peggy probably asked. Out of concern."

"Whatever."

"I'd be freaked if it happened to me," he said.

"Well, it didn't, did it?"

"Sorry," he muttered. "See ya."

I watched him turn away. "Hey, Sharp," I called when he reached the driveway.

"Yeah?"

"I didn't mean to be so snippy. I guess maybe I am a little rattled. It happened so quickly. And everything's such a mess."

"It's okay, Jane. I didn't take it personally."

But I wondered if he had, because his eyes looked withdrawn.

If at first you don't succeed, try, try again. So I did. I wrote yet another letter to Bubba.

> *Dear Bubba,*
> *How did you get my address? This is*
> *supposed to be a one-way street. My way.*
> *So go away.*
>
> > *In absolute control,*
> > *Gabriel*

Failure. I drew a big X across that one, stuffed it into my Bubba folder, and crammed the folder into my drawer.

I'd come with Dad to the marina. He went into his office, a trailer brought onto the property since the fire, to look for some blueprints. Sitting on the pier, bathed in the soft yellow glow of the waning moon, I tossed a twig into the bayou and watched it swirl before it slowly drifted away. A night bird was crying in the trees. I yanked my Bubba folder out of my backpack, which was lying on the dock beside me.

> *Dear Bubba,*
> *What exactly do you want from me?*
> *I have nothing to offer you, and you*
> *certainly can't offer me much.*
>
> > *Empty-handed,*
> > *Gabriel*

It wasn't really what I wanted to say. I scribbled through it and stashed it with the others. Having bared my soul to Bubba since second grade, I suddenly found myself at a loss for words. Me? At a loss for words? Who ever thought that day would come?

"Your dress for the dance is so pretty," said Carmella as I twirled in front of the mirror. "I can't believe you got it at a secondhand store."

"Me either," said Harmony.

"Only nine dollars, but I have to make some adjustments." It was a red dress with clean lines. No frills, no lace, no beads or buttons.

"Sharp's gonna love it," said Harmony.

"Yeah, he probably will," I said with a smile. "At least by the time I get through with it."

"The color's perfect for you," added Harmony.

"It's so weird you're going out with Sharp," Carmella said.

"He's *such* a brother. I can't imagine going out with *him*," said Harmony.

"But you can imagine going out with Zander, can't you?" asked Carmella mischievously. "And he's a brother."

Harmony blushed and kicked Carmella's leg.

"I already know you're hot for Zander," I said.

"You told her?" Harmony said to Carmella.

"That shouldn't surprise you," I said. "Neither of you can keep a secret. But really, Harmony, Zander? He's such a squab!"

"He's not so bad," said Harmony, but her smile gave her away.

"You seriously need to get out more, Harmony. It's that homeschool thing. . . . You've severely limited your choices. When you get to high school, you won't believe the possibilities."

"I'm about quality, not quantity."

"Quality? You two are way too sheltered. Zander and Jason Blackshire? At least have some imagination."

"You're going out with Sharp. What's the difference?" asked Carmella, defending her friend.

"It's not a real date," I said, wondering if it actually was a real date.

"Sharp thinks you're pretty," said Harmony.

"He does?"

"That's what he told Chord. I heard him. They didn't know I was there."

"In other words, you were spying again," I accused her.

"Not spying. *Observing.*"

"That's like calling thieving 'borrowing.' Doesn't work for me. You two are the biggest snoops in the galaxy."

"We are merely curious," said Carmella. "Come on, Harmony. Let's go."

The two of them disappeared, probably in search of someone to "observe."

I dug Aunt Jane's sewing kit from the closet and altered the dress to make it perfect. I tried to visualize the expressions on the faces of Raphael and Emma when I sashayed into the homecoming dance.

If it hadn't been for that mail-in rebate that came with the cosmetics I bought, I probably never would have seen it. I went into Dad's home office for a postage stamp, and there, on the desk, atop of a stack of manila envelopes, was a sheaf of papers stapled together. By the letterhead, I saw that it was a report from the insurance company. I lifted the cover letter and browsed through the forms and documents beneath. And there it was, midway down the third page, in the square labeled "Ignition point": "Kitchen—grease fire—fryer left on." My hands began to shake as I leafed through the remaining papers. Nowhere did my name appear, at least not prominently enough to catch my scanning eye. I exhaled with relief. It was logical—if I wasn't named in an official legal document, then I wasn't to blame.

Once again I tried to compose a letter to Bubba that would accurately convey my feelings.

> Dear Bubba,
>   Your letter was inappropriate. An invasion. Like a solicitor on the telephone. Like an eavesdropper. Like a burglar.
>   Get a life,
>   Gabriel
>
> P.S. Like a disease.

Bubba Crosses the Line

Chord met me on the porch. "Sharp's teaching a lesson," he said. "That means we have thirty minutes."

"This is getting old," I complained. "Sneaking a moment here and there. We have to find a better way."

"I agree, but for now, I'll take what I can get. Come on." We walked across the deMichaels' backyard and climbed the ladder to the tree house.

I opened the mailbox. Only one envelope occupied it. I reached for it and gasped, because even though I'd only seen it once before, I immediately recognized the handwriting. I looked up and down the street as if I expected my imaginary enemy to be lurking nearby. Then I slowly tore away the flap and unfolded the paper inside.

> Dear Gabriel,
>   Don't you think it's time we met face

to face? Waffle House. Wednesday at
seven. Booth four. Be there.

By invitation only,
Bubba

Yikes! I'd certainly never imagined anything like this.
Bubba in the flesh? Did Bubba have flesh? What was appropriate attire for meeting your imaginary enemy?

Once again I couldn't sleep. I rolled over and pulled the blan-
kets up to my chin. Through the window I stared at the cres-
cent moon, faceless and bored, hanging in the sky. I replayed
the events of the night of the fire, as I had done countless
times. I remembered serving that last hungry customer, a
middle-school-age boy with braces and a gold hoop in one ear
who knew Carmella and Harmony from their homeschool
network. Then Zander and I had cleaned up, him tackling
the heavier tasks such as folding up serving tables and taking
the trash to the Dumpster. I'd put away the condiments and
spices, cleaned pots and utensils, and washed the ceramic
liner of the Crock-Pot. I didn't specifically remember turning
off the fryer, but who remembers incidental things such as
flushing the toilet and hanging up the phone? No one, that's
who. But that doesn't mean those things weren't done.

I *did* turn off the fryer. I was meticulous and methodi-
cal. I would never have been that careless.

I turned away from the window and flipped my pillow
over. Bubba was freaking me out . . . writing these
unasked-for letters and invading my head space. "I've
about had enough of you, Bubba," I said aloud. "Take your
spooky tricks elsewhere."

Reality Check

I poured the batter into the pan and slipped the pan into the oven. Then, as I cleaned the mixing bowls, spoons, and measuring cups, I thought about Bubba and the letters I'd received.

I'd known Bubba most of my life, and he'd never done anything like this before. Come to think of it, he'd never done *anything* before. Which was exactly the way it was supposed to be.

Bubba didn't write those letters. He couldn't, considering his status—nonexistent. This whole thing had to be one of those strange dreams that somehow tangles itself up with real life.

I dashed down the hall to my room, where I unearthed my Bubba folder from a pile of stuff on my dresser. When I flipped it open, fantasy collided with reality like a speeding truck slamming into a telephone pole. Because there, in the left-hand pocket, lurked those haunting messages.

This is insane, I thought. Absolutely insane. I removed the stack of letters from the right-hand pocket. They were the ones I'd written to Bubba over the years, from second grade to the present, covering a variety of my personal disasters and defeats. There must have been more than a hundred. I read them one by one, looking for some clue as to what had awakened Bubba from hibernation. Had I inadvertently summoned him? But nothing I read looked to me like grounds for Bubba to suddenly become assertive.

Could it have been something I did? Some accident or prank? The fire, maybe? Or was Bubba misinterpreting some of my actions—reading them at face value without peering beneath the surface?

"Jane! Your cake," called Zander from the kitchen.

"Oh no!" I jumped up and ran to the oven. The timer was buzzing away like the honeybees Elliot had recorded at the blueberry farm. I grabbed a pot holder and opened the oven door. Then I muttered a short string of those inappropriate French words. The cake was flat and round and nearly black.

Zander leaned beside me to peer into the oven. "Least you didn't catch the house on fire."

"Zander, shut your trap."

"I hope that's not all you're planning for Dad's birthday party, because he doesn't need an oversized hockey puck."

"You're just hilarious." I yanked the mixing bowl out of the cabinet. "Back to the drawing board. Hey, Zander, go borrow three eggs from the deMichaels. Please?"

I reread that second letter from Bubba. Over and over and over. I reached for my pen and a sheet of loose-leaf.

> Dear Bubba,
>   First of all, I'm not sure I want to meet you in person. This whole thing has

become very eerie. You're imaginary,
remember, so the very fact that I'd even
consider meeting you puts my sanity in
dangerous territory. Get it?

Secondly, if I do agree to meet you,
and that's a big if, it certainly will not be
at Waffle House. That would be far too
complicated and uncomfortable. A public
place, however, is a good idea, as you
could be just as dangerous and unstable
as some online pervert.

Cautiously,
Gabriel

When we reached my driveway, Chord glanced around
nervously before taking my hand and gazing into my eyes.
We talked, our faces close together, and the energy between us palpable. He gave me a hug. His hand lingered
on my waist. "Bye, Chord," I called, blowing him a kiss as
I opened the front door.

Bubba Strikes Again

Yet another letter from Bubba arrived the Saturday of the homecoming dance. I stood in my bedroom, freshly showered, with a towel wrapped around me and my hair dripping. That was when Carmella came in. "You got a letter," she said. I froze, realizing immediately that there was only one person I'd received mail from lately. (Person?) Like I needed this now! Like I wasn't nervous enough about going to the dance with Sharp! Did everything have to happen at once? I tore the envelope open and tossed it away, anxiously unfolding the page inside.

Dear Gabriel,
    Because I know you are a curious girl,
I'm certain you won't be able to resist the
urge to meet me in person in spite of your
reservations. I do understand your desire
to choose a public location (although I can
assure you that I am harmless), as well as

your reluctance for such an event to occur
in your place of employment. I have
another suggestion—someplace neutral.
The nonfiction floor of the public library—
the Mercury Boulevard branch. The tables
by the windows behind the psychology
books (the one hundreds in the Dewey
decimal system) would be perfect. Five-
thirty Thursday works for me. I look
forward to seeing you.

Your imaginary enemy,
Bubba

I read and reread the letter. What kind of an imaginary enemy would choose a library as a meeting place? Then I thought about all those books, stuffed to the gills with fictional characters, and decided that maybe the library was an obvious choice. But why the psychology section? Wouldn't the fiction section have been more appropriate?

Then I almost threw up. Psychology! I'm going crazy. I'm losing my mind. I'm slipping over the edge, and there's no sliding back. I sank to the floor, panicked and threatened.

"Aren't you getting ready? Sharp is. I just got off the phone with Harmony, and she said he was taking a shower." Carmella was standing in the doorway. I don't know how long I had been sitting there in a daze.

"What time is it?"

"Six-thirty."

"Oh drat! We're leaving at seven." I jumped up and looked in the mirror, which may have been a bad move. My hair was clumpy and damp, and my face was splotchy.

"What's with the black nail polish?" asked Carmella.

I resisted the urge to call her a squab. "It completes the look," I said matter-of-factly. "I wonder what Chord's doing tonight?"

Carmella looked up at me, puzzled. "What difference does it make?"

"None. I was just wondering, that's all. . . . Do you think he'll like my outfit?"

"Chord? What do you—" She glanced at my dress hanging on the closet door and gaped. "Oh no, Jane. What happened to it?"

"I fixed it," I said. "I told you I was going to make some adjustments."

"But Jane . . . it's . . . um . . . it's . . . well, it's like the Barbies."

"Yeah, I know. Isn't it great?" Originally a scarlet dress with a fitted bodice and gracefully flared skirt, my gown was now slashed and studded and totally punkified. I'd ripped one sleeve from a black lace blouse and attached it with a tightly spaced row of silver safety pins. The outer skirt was torn into narrow strips, knotted at the ends. I was too modest to slice the lining as well. A heavy black zipper snaked like railroad tracks across the chest. Brass studs and ruby rhinestones were scattered in constellations over the fabric.

"So what about Chord? Do you think he'll like it?"

Carmella stared at me. "Chord? Who cares . . . Sharp's your date. Jane, what are you putting in your hair?"

"It's temporary dye. I'm doing blue streaks. Blue is Sharp's favorite color. I wonder what Chord's favorite color is?"

"Who cares?" Carmella's frustration was rearing its ugly head. "Are you really going to wear that dress?"

"Yeah. Is my hair spiky enough?"

She shook her head in despair.

"Carmella," a voice called.

"Harmony, get in here. Now. My sister's lost her mind."

"Hello, Harmony. Hand me that black leather vest on my dresser," I said as I pulled on a pair of fishnets.

"You're wearing that, Jane?" Harmony asked.

"Yeah. You like it?"

For a while she just stood there with her mouth hanging open. Finally, she touched my hair and said, "You can't go out like this. Sharp looks . . . normal."

"I shoulda pierced my lip," I said.

Carmella moaned. "I told you she's gone crazy."

"Carmella, I'm not having a Meltdown. Or if I am, then it's a good thing. Way overdue."

"Poor Sharp," muttered Harmony. "He's in for a shock."

"Well, what do you think?" I asked, pirouetting in front of the mirror. I didn't look remotely like the Jane everyone knew, but I definitely had style for the first time in my life. Not the style Trina or Emma would choose, but style, definitely style.

"Sharp's gonna croak," said Harmony.

"This is a really bad idea," said Carmella.

"It was your idea, remember?"

My little sister planted her hands on her hips. "This was *not* my idea, Jane. Don't try to blame it on me."

"Blame? Oh brother, Carmella, you deserve praise."

"Just keep my name out of it," she shouted.

I blew kisses to Voodoo Raphael, the Barbies, and the Gothosaurs. "Wish me luck," I sang to them, and left the room with Carmella and Harmony in my wake.

Zander and Jazz saw me first. "Whoa, Jane, you're all punked out," said Jazz as he jumped off Zander's bed and ran into the hallway.

Zander dropped his guitar and followed. His eyes bugged out. "Yikes! What happened to the Hollister look?" he asked.

"I wasn't feeling it," I said. "You like?"

"Fabulous," said Jazz.

"Totally awesome," added Zander. "But I'm not sure Mom and Dad will agree."

I walked into the living room. Stupidly, I hadn't anticipated the family plan. My clan and Sharp's were gathered there like our date was some newsworthy event. Sharp was standing next to Dad, looking more traditional than he had since the day three years earlier when I'd joined the homeschool brigade's field trip to the courthouse.

My mother's face paled when she caught sight of me. "Her dress didn't look like that when I saw it," I heard her explain to Peggy.

"Nor did her hair," added Dad.

For a fleeting moment, Elliot studied me like he'd never seen me before. Then he smiled and winked and I relaxed a little.

Chord was sitting on the sofa. "Yo, Cinderella, the

glass slippers really make the outfit," he said, gesturing toward my violet patent-leather platforms with five-inch heels. I couldn't decide if it was scorn or admiration I saw in his eyes.

Sharp grinned and grabbed my hand. "Wow, Jane. You look great!" And even though I knew everyone else thought I'd gone bananas, I realized Sharp was dazzled. And I was so taken with him that I forget to wonder how Raphael looked that night or what his reaction to seeing me at the dance would be.

"Hi, Emma."

She looked at me for a second, a puzzled expression on her face. "Jane!" She fingered the one sleeve of my garment. "You look . . . Wow, I'm stunned. I never imagined you dressed like that. And I didn't know you were coming."

"My little surprise. This is Sharp."

"Hi. We've met before. The homeschool brigade, right?" Emma teased.

"Homeschool brigade?" asked Sharp.

I winked at Emma, turned to Sharp, and said, "Let's go dance."

"You sure you want to dance with the 'little neighbor boy'?"

"Positive. Come on."

Kids from school hardly recognized me with my blue hair and black eyeliner. It made the evening much more adventurous. And the fact that my date was a tall stranger only increased their curiosity.

Raphael and Trina were suddenly standing next to me. "Rafi," I said, breezing a casual kiss on his cheek. "You sure look handsome. And isn't Trina lovely?" She looked like a model in a tight black dress (predictable choice) and stiletto heels, but she must have been trashed, because her makeup was smeared and her face seemed wilted. She kept giggling, stumbling about, and bumping into things.

"Jane?" Rafi was looking at me like he wasn't certain who I was.

"Don't tell me you don't remember me?" I teased.

"Course I remember you. You look different, that's all."

"This is Sharp," I said. I grabbed Sharp's hand. "I love this song. See you later, Rafi." Sharp twined his fingers through mine and I felt tingly all over. You've heard that bit about hindsight being twenty-twenty. It's funny how when you reflect on something once it's over and done, your perspective is totally different than it is while events are unfolding. Looking back, I'm not sure why I ever thought Raphael was so great. We had fun together, but I don't think either of us tried terribly hard to really get to know the other deep inside. After he dumped me, it was less his companionship I missed and more the status of having a boyfriend and the fun of hanging out as a foursome—Emma, Tony, Raphael, and me. Of course, my pride was wounded. That was what really stung—knowing that when Trina walked into the picture, I became invisible. I suddenly realized I didn't care what Raphael thought about my attire or my escort. I only wanted to be with Sharp.

On the ride home, I kept wondering what to do. Would he kiss me? I hoped so. Should I kiss him? I wanted to. How did people go from being childhood playmates to something else?

"I had a great time, even if you didn't really want to be with me," Sharp said, jolting me out of my reverie.

"What are you talking about?" I asked.

"Carmella and Harmony told me about your boyfriend."

Yet again I wanted to annihilate those two blabber-mouths. "Ex-boyfriend. I don't care about him, Sharp."

"It's okay, Jane. I knew what this date was about. But I hadn't anticipated having so much—"

"But you've got it wrong," I protested. Then I did the boldest thing I've ever done. I leaned over and kissed him right on the mouth. I felt the car swerve. "I wanted to be with you," I said, pulling away.

Sharp watched the road. Silence filled the car. I felt shattered—like I'd been really stupid and once again couldn't fix it.

"Sharp?"

Still he said nothing.

"Talk to me!" I cried.

He glanced at me, then back at the road. "I have feelings, you know, Jane. I don't want you making a joke of me."

I touched his arm. "Sharp, I'm not. I wouldn't do that. I like you. A lot. Please believe me."

He turned onto our street.

"Sharp. I'm serious."

"I want to believe you," he said, pulling over to the curb and turning off the car. "But it scares me. I don't want to be a pawn in some game."

"What?"

"You know what I mean. . . . I'm just the boy next door you can use to get at Raphael."

"It's not like that, Sharp. You're seeing what you want to see. Not what's really there."

He sat motionless, looking straight ahead, drumming his fingers on the steering wheel. I couldn't think of anything to say, so I leaned over and kissed him again. This time, after only a moment's resistance, Sharp kissed me back. And I'd never been kissed like that before.

Setting the Stage

"How was the dance, Jane?" Mom asked at breakfast. "Fine." I rubbed my head. My hair, freshly shampooed, still held a hint of blue spray.

"Did Sharp have fun?"

"I guess."

"Well, was it a date, or just friends, or what?"

"Mom," I said in a bored voice, but my heart was thumping wildly.

She winked at Dad across the table. "That must mean it was a date."

"Sharp must have horrible taste," said Zander. "He must be desperate."

"What would you know, Lysander?" I retorted.

"I can't believe *you* wore that awesome dress. You're usually so . . . normal."

"Ugh!" I said, leaving the table. Once again, Zander calling me normal felt like an insult.

"Harmony told me Sharp went off with Elliot early this morning. They went to record waves on the beach," Carmella said.

"Really?" I answered with feigned disinterest.

"Yep. Sharp loves those recording adventures as much as Elliot does. He even plans some of them."

"Figures. . . . What about Chord?"

"What about him?"

"Did he go with them?"

"No."

"So what's he doing?"

Carmella looked at me quizzically. "I'm not sure. . . . Hanging around the house, I guess. Why?"

"No reason." I smiled secretively.

"What's the deal with you and Chord?" she asked with a hint of disgust in her voice.

"Nothing," I replied smugly. "I can't imagine what you're talking about."

Chord and I met on the deMichaels' porch. We sat beside each other on the steps, and he threw his arm around my shoulders. We talked quietly and I rested my hand on his knee. He reached over and stroked my hair. When I got up to leave, he pulled me to himself and kissed my face.

I listened for the sound of Elliot's van. Midafternoon, he and Sharp pulled into the driveway. I watched from the porch as Sharp unloaded recording equipment. He carried an armload of speakers and wires to the garage. Then another. And another. He finally closed the van doors and crossed the yard.

"Hi, Jane." He looked shy and tenative.

"Hi. How's it going?"

"Okay. Want to go for a walk?"

"Sure."

"Hey, Sharp, do you know what you're getting yourself into?" Zander called from the doorway. "She's poison!"

Sharp laughed. "I'll take my chances."

"This is awkward," I said.

"What do you mean?"

"Both of our families are on alert—watching everything we do—speculating."

Sharp grinned. "Yeah, I know. All day Elliot kept fishing about last night. Asking all kinds of questions."

"What'd you tell him?"

"I dunno. That I had a good time. That I liked being with you."

"You did?"

"Yeah. What'd you tell your family?"

"I was evasive."

"Why?"

"I don't know. It's just weird. You're like . . . Sharp. Like the boy next door."

"I am the boy next door."

"I know. That's why it's weird."

"Raphael called me this morning," Emma said when I answered the phone.

"Oh, yeah. Why?"

"He wanted the dirt on Sharp."

"What'd you tell him?"

"Not much. I don't know much."

"Did he roll the R in Sharp?"

"Actually, I think he did."

"Figures. At least he's consistent. He can roll his Rs til he's lead dog in the nursing home and I wouldn't care."

Emma laughed.

"I can't believe I thought it was sexy. It's fake, anyhow. He took Spanish One in ninth grade and thinks he's Antonio Banderas."

"Jane, you crack me up. So is your new look a one-time thing, or a lifestyle?"

"Neither. From now on, I'll just follow my whims. No point in swapping one label for another."

"What label?"

"*Normal*. Just ask Zander."

"Jane. I'd never have labeled you normal," she said.

"Remember when you said I wasn't a real slacker?"

"Did I say that?"

"Yeah. Freshman year. Well, I've decided you're right. I'm not a slacker. I'm simply very efficient."

"Efficient?"

"Right. I don't waste my time on unprofitable efforts. Like school. I conserve my energy for more worthwhile pursuits."

"Hmmm . . . I think maybe *slacker* was the right term after all, Jane."

"Bye, Emma. Chord's at the door."

"Chord?"

"Yeah. Long story. I'll update you later. Bye."

Chord waited until Carmella and Harmony left the room. Then he grabbed my arm. "Sharp isn't suspicious, is he?" he asked.

"Shhh. Don't talk so loud."

"Well, is he?"

"Shhh. I don't think so."

Chord took my hands in his. "I don't want him to get hurt. Regardless of you and me, he's my brother."

"I know. This is difficult."

"What are we going to do?" He pulled me against him and pressed his lips to my neck. I felt the warmth of his breath on my flesh and couldn't come up with an answer.

Blind Date

I'd been uncertain what to wear to meet Bubba. I wondered what he was expecting. Glamour and glitz? Leather and lace? Business casual? Punked out? Denim? Waffle House uniform?

Because whatever Bubba wanted was just the way I *didn't* want to dress. I wasn't the sort of girl who dressed to please an imaginary enemy. So I settled on my favorite worn-out pair of jeans, my Marvin the Martian T-shirt, and my running shoes. Just in case I needed to make a break for it.

I walked into the library, glancing around. I spied no one familiar on the ground floor. A man walked by pushing a cart of books. "Where's nonfiction? The one hundreds in the Dewey decimal system?" I asked.

"Third floor," he replied, and gestured toward the stairs. "Or you can ride the elevator."

I climbed the stairs and looked around. I hadn't spent much time in libraries. I pulled Bubba's letter from my pocket. What in the world was the Dewey decimal system? I vaguely remembered my third-grade teacher talking about it. Was it some way of converting percentages into fractions? No. It had something to do with those numbers on the spines of library books, but I wasn't sure what. Did Bubba think I was a librarian or something? I didn't even have a library card.

"Where are the one hundreds?" I whispered to the lady behind the desk.

"Over there. That entire section."

"Thanks." I walked to the area she'd indicated and followed the aisle to the large plate-glass windows. Six tables were lined up, all occupied. I rechecked Bubba's letter. He hadn't specified which table. I stepped back into the narrow aisle between the stacks to evaluate the crop of potential Bubbas. At the first table sat three people who looked like college students. They were comparing notes and drawing diagrams. Next was a frazzled mother with twins sleeping in a stroller. There were several parenting books spread out on the table. At the third sat a woman around my mother's age typing on a laptop. The fourth was inhabited by two preteenage boys giggling at paintings of naked women in art books. One of them saw me and blushed. At the fifth, a guy in a sloppy hat and tattered jacket sat facing the window. I wondered if he was a homeless person seeking refuge from the world outside. At the final table sat a couple who should have been in the anatomy section, judging by their behavior.

I reasoned that if Bubba was there, he had to be either the laptop woman or the sloppy hat guy. He'd said nothing about bringing along friends, and the other tables were all occupied by more than one person. I stood between two rows of bookshelves, unsure. The laptop woman looked up and smiled.

"Excuse me, are you meeting someone here?" I asked her.

"No, dear."

"Sorry."

I looked at the sloppy hat guy. The set of his shoulders seemed familiar. I stepped toward him. He was idly flipping through the pages of a book about volcanoes. "Excuse me," I said, standing behind him. My heart was beating rapidly.

He closed the book, turned, and removed his hat. "Gabriel, you came. I was afraid you might chicken out," he said, his smile bright and open. "I'm Bubba." He extended his hand, and like a fool I shook it.

"You?" I was confused, embarrassed, shocked. And, I'll admit, angry.

"Me."

"But . . . ?"

"Who were you expecting?"

"I . . . um . . . well, I didn't know who . . . but I never thought . . . What are *you* doing here?"

"Meeting you face to face, just like I proposed in the letter."

"What?" I was rattled, trying to merge the person before me with the Bubba I'd corresponded with since childhood. "Nice disguise," I said sarcastically.

"I thought you'd like it."

"I was lying. It sucks." I folded my arms over my chest. "Well?"

"Let me explain," he said somewhat formally, like this was a business meeting.

"That might be a good plan."

I thought back to when I was little—to the time I got my first kiss, the one Sharp planted on my cheek while Chord ridiculed us with taunts about love. I remembered how I had repeatedly rubbed my face, but that darned kiss just wouldn't disappear. I had wiped it with my fingers and dabbed at it with my shirt and scrubbed it with a soapy washcloth, but it had remained plastered to my cheek. For all I knew it was still there, staining my flesh with its invisible tattoo.

That was how I felt standing in the psychology section of the library facing Bubba for the first time. Except instead of a kiss, it was a slap, and nothing could take away the sting.

"Well, start explaining," I said, sitting across the table from him. There was not a hint of warmth in my voice or a spark of welcome in my eyes.

"Keep your voice down, Gabriel. This *is* a library, you know."

I realized I had spoken rather loudly. "Fine. Start explaining," I hissed in a dramatic whisper. Then I added, "Bubba," with a sneer as I leaned back and crossed my arms.

"You're angry."

"Well, duh." I spoke louder than I had intended. A few heads turned to look in our direction.

"Maybe we should go to the courtyard. We're disturbing people."

"Don't you mean *I'm* disturbing people? Isn't that what you mean?" I said, my voice rising a pitch with each word.

"Come on," he said.

He walked around the table toward me and reached for my chair. I sprang from my seat. "I don't need your help, *Bubba*."

I whirled past him and stomped down the stairs, leaving him in my wake. At the back of my mind the strangest thing was happening. I was wondering what numbers the Dewey decimal system assigned to cookbooks. Were there many cookbooks in the library, and did they get checked out often? Maybe food splatter stains embellished their pages. Did they include nutritional facts and calorie counts? Could I find a profitable new dish to prepare for the next fishing tournament? Whoa, I told myself. I think you've lost your mind—truly slipped into the twilight zone between sanity and madness.

"Are you okay?" Bubba asked when I reached the landing. I snapped back to reality.

"Define *okay*," I replied acidly.

We sat at a small table in the corner of the courtyard. "Jane—"

"Don't you mean Gabriel, Bubba?" I shifted so that I was sitting sideways, turning my head to glare at him over my right shoulder. I crossed my arms and smirked with false casualness.

"Okay then, Gabriel . . . this is what happened." He paused, as if he wasn't sure where to start.

I jumped in. "I can't wait to hear, and it better be good."

His eyes met mine, making my heart lurch. "Remember the day you asked me to the dance?"

"Yes, Sharp . . . I mean *Bubba* . . . yes, Bubba, I remember. We all have our moments of desperation. What does that have to do with this?"

"You stacked your books with my sheet music on top of my saxophone case. Remember?"

"Not really. Not exactly the highlight of my life, you know . . . where I put my school stuff. Slackers like me don't concern ourselves with such trivialities."

"Well, your stuff was piled with mine, and when you picked it up you left your folder with my music books."

"Crime of the century? Big deal. Call in the National Guard."

"It wasn't a crime," he said softly, as if my sarcasm offended him. "Just a forgotten folder."

"So?"

"I didn't realize it was there. I wasn't exactly thinking about folders. I was thinking about going out with you. Excited about going out with you. I've always liked you—ever since I can remember." I rolled my eyes just like Demonseed rolls his *R*s. Sharp looked away, then back at me. "Later that night, when I went to practice my pieces, I saw it there—that blue folder. And it had 'Bubba, Letters to my Imaginary Enemy' written on the front. I thought it was Chord's. Maybe some assignment for his creative writing class. I opened it and started reading those letters. That's when I knew it was actually your folder. Your letters."

"Which you kept reading?" I accused him. "You're worse than Carmella and Harmony."

"I did keep reading. Wouldn't you have? I *know* you would."

"Maybe," I admitted grudgingly.

"Anyway, I thought it was really cool that you'd written all those Bubba letters over the years. I liked the way your handwriting matured, and your rages, too. And then I thought about how you always called my family weird, because of Elliot's projects and stuff, and I was glad you were kind of weird, too."

"*You're* calling *me* weird?"

"Well, it is a bit weird, Jane. Having an imaginary enemy. Writing letters to him."

I tossed my head. "Oh, and who are you to judge?"

"That's what you don't get—I'm not judging." His voice was quiet, almost as if he was talking to himself. He leaned closer to me. "I liked it. It made me more attracted to you than ever. Like you weren't the conventional girl you pretended to be. That's why I was so turned on by what you wore to the dance. It exposed the artist in you."

"Artist? I'm no artist."

"In the broad sense of the word you are."

"Whatever. You still shouldn't have read my letters."

"I couldn't *not* read them, Jane. But here's the odd thing: I was jealous of Bubba."

I became aware of his hands on the tabletop, fidgeting nervously. "How could you be jealous of Bubba?" I asked incredulously. "He doesn't exist!"

"But in a way he does. As much as any other intangible."

"I don't even know what you're talking about," I said in exasperation.

He continued. "So I went next door—you weren't home. I hung out with Zander and Jazz, and snuck into your room to stash your folder back with your stuff—"

I turned to face him squarely, my eyes aflame. I expected him to flinch, but he didn't. "What? You snooped around my room?"

"No. I didn't snoop. Just put your letters on a pile of stuff. Then last week, I did it again. It was easy. Your folder was sitting on your bed with your French book. So I read the new letters you'd written to Bubba and planned this meeting."

"You make rank amateurs of our snoopy little sisters. You invaded my privacy."

At least he had the grace to look ashamed. "I'm sorry. I never meant to hurt you. I was intrigued. It didn't seem so awful at the time."

"All that still doesn't explain what you're doing here dressed in some funky coat pretending to be my imaginary enemy."

Sharp inhaled. "Remember how Harmony and Carmella told me you only asked me out to get back at your boyfriend? I wrote those Bubba letters to you to . . . I don't know why . . . to get your attention, I guess. And share a secret with you. But then, at the dance, it was so nice being with you, and you said you liked being with me, and I wasn't sure what to do. But I'd already asked you to meet me, so here we are."

I raised one eyebrow a bit, wishing I could knock him down a few pegs by doing a full-fledged Mrs. Perkins.

He reached across the table, grabbed my hand, and looked into my eyes. "Is it really so bad? What I did? Didn't you kind of like it? The mystery? The magic? The risk?"

"You invaded my privacy."

"Yeah, I did. But by accident. Only because your stuff got mixed up with mine. It's not like I went digging through your closet or something."

"That doesn't excuse it."

"And I had no evil intent. I wanted to tease you, maybe. Entice you. But that's it."

"You conspired against me with my imaginary enemy," I accused him.

"I wouldn't really call it a conspiracy, Jane. Bubba's imaginary. And it's not like the CIA and Department of Homeland Security were involved."

We sat in silence. I wasn't totally mad now that I knew the whole story. It was even rather funny. And Sharp was right—I had enjoyed the mystery, magic, and risk. It wasn't as if he was ridiculing me for having an imaginary enemy. He liked it—liked me better for it. I sighed. "At least you aren't an online pervert."

He smiled and it melted my heart. "Well, Gabriel, do you forgive me?"

At first I didn't say anything, due to my stubborn streak. "So Bubba," I finally asked, "do you want to go get a soda?"

"Does that mean we're okay with each other?"

"Yeah," I said, smiling. "But from now on, leave my private papers alone, understand?"

"Yeah, I understand."

"And when I need an enemy, you'll be on the receiving end. Got it?"

"Got it. But please don't call me Bubba. Unless you kiss me. Then you can call me anything."

"Okay, Bubba," I said mischievously.

Salt

I closed the door to the dishwasher and turned it on. My father was wiping the counters. I touched his arm. "Hey, Dad?"

"Yes, Jane?"

"Um . . . I . . . well, I've thought about it a lot . . . a whole lot . . . like every spare minute . . . and well . . . I think maybe they were right."

"They who?"

"The firefighters." I clasped my hands together. "That night . . . I was tired and preoccupied. I'm pretty sure I forgot to unplug the fryer. That's what I usually do . . . unplug it just to be certain."

"It could happen to anyone," my father said softly. "Everyone makes mistakes. But I appreciate you owning up to your part."

"I feel horrible about it, Dad. I'm so sorry. I'll do whatever it takes to make things better."

"Jane, accidents happen. I've done similar things myself. This time the consequences were severe, but still, it could have been worse."

"Will you ever forgive me?"

He pulled me against him and hugged me. "I love you, Janie. There's nothing to forgive. It's over. Done. Construction on the new building starts next week. We've all moved on. I think it's time for you to do the same."

"I'm trying." I closed the cabinet doors and pushed the chairs beneath the table. "So Dad, if you didn't have us kids to mess things up, your life would be perfect."

"What are you talking about?" he asked.

"You love Mom, your job, you have the *Annika Elise*. Everything you want. But then we do stuff . . . like the fire, and things aren't so great anymore."

"Sit down, little girl," he said. Calling me "little girl" meant he found my thinking very young.

"What?" I asked defensively as I slid into a chair.

He sat across from me. "Hmmm . . . how can I make you understand?" He picked up the salt shaker and rolled it between his hands. "You like to cook, right?"

"Yeah."

"And when you bake cookies or cake or pastry, you shovel in some sweetener, right?"

"Yeah."

"But you put in something else, too, don't you, to balance it out."

"What? Flour?"

"No, Jane, not flour. Salt. Without it, the cookies or cake would be too sweet. Almost every sweet recipe has a bit of salt."

"So?"

"Well, first of all, my children are the sweet in my life. I want you to know that. But I'm glad they come with a little salt. Without it, it would be hard to appreciate the sweet things."

"So you don't mind when we mess up?"

"It can be hard, really hard, to watch your kids make mistakes, but *everyone* makes mistakes. I might not like some of the things you do, just like you don't like everything I do, but I can accept your mistakes. I hope you can accept mine."

"I feel really bad about that fire, Dad."

He reached across the table to squeeze my hand. "It bothers me more that you're sometimes unkind to your siblings, Jane. So if you need to obsess about something, consider that."

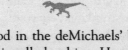

Chord and I stood in the deMichaels' backyard, talking quietly and occasionally laughing. He took my hand and stepped even nearer to me. Sharp's voice shattered the moment. "So Harmony and Carmella were right about you two." He stalked across the yard toward us.

Chord and I pulled away from each other in shock. "Sharp," I said. I took a step toward him, but he moved away.

"And you—my brother. I can't believe this," he snarled at Chord.

"Sharp, just listen," I pleaded.

"I don't want to listen to either of you—you traitors. You cheats." He snatched a fistful of Chord's shirt.

"Sharp, no!" I cried. He pushed Chord, who stumbled backward. Then Chord lunged at Sharp, and the two of them were punching each other and grunting. Carmella and Harmony emerged from behind Elliot's van, all big-eyed and frightened. At thirteen, they still believed only what they wanted to about what they saw and heard. The rest they embellished at will.

Chord escaped from Sharp's grasp, whirled around, and tried to catch him in a stranglehold. Sharp eluded him and punched him, connecting with his shoulder because Chord attempted to dodge the incoming blow.

"Make them stop," pleaded Harmony. She grabbed my arm. "Do something. Please."

The guys were now on the ground, a tangle of fists and elbows. I moved to pull them apart, but when I got close to them Chord reared back and nearly knocked me over. I backed away, afraid I'd get hurt. "Get the hose," I said frantically. "That's what you do with dogs."

"The hose?" Harmony looked puzzled, and then ran toward the faucet. I watched her fumble with the nozzle while Carmella urged her to hurry.

Suddenly I started to laugh. I couldn't stop. The sight of them so distraught was priceless. I clutched my sides and gasped for breath. The boys joined me in my hysterics. Soon the three of us were exchanging high fives and embracing each other to keep from falling to the ground. Carmella and Harmony stood there dumbfounded.

Sharp finally recovered enough of his self-control to call out, "Oh, Harmony. Carmella. The jig's up!"

"Huh?" Harmony asked.

"Did you like our choreography, you little snoops?" yelled Chord.

Sharp wrapped his arm around my waist. I could feel the warmth of his hand through my shirt. The two spies shamefacedly gaped at us. "Sharp, you saw them," said Harmony. "They were fooling around behind your back just like we told you. We saw them bunches of times. They even kissed. Jane was cheating on you with your own brother."

"Why are you holding Jane?" Carmella asked him. "Aren't you mad?"

"Furious," said Sharp, laughing while he hugged me to his chest.

"But they cheated on you," insisted Harmony, sneering at Chord and me.

"Get over it, Harmony," said Sharp.

"We set you up, lame brains," said Chord, catching his breath. "We found your dirty little notebook, so we thought we'd give you something juicy to write about. But you two sorry sneaks couldn't stand it, could you? This was just too scandalous to keep to yourselves, so you turned tattletale and ran to poor Sharp."

"To save him from us," I added.

"You and Chord were faking it?" Harmony asked.

"Exactly. You know Chord's not my type."

"Or Jane mine . . . not that she's not fine, but—"

"Why?" asked Harmony, totally confused.

"Why? Why do you think? We're on to your psycho little game, and we turned it on you."

"That was mean," said Carmella. "Really mean."

I couldn't believe her nerve. "What? You two *spied* on us. All of us. And as if that wasn't bad enough, you took notes! You'd best keep your big mouths shut."

"And stay out of my way," said Chord.

"Yeah," said Sharp. "Next time we won't be so amused.

Next time we'll come at you with our teeth bared. And we've seen you running around the neighborhood with Jason Blackshire and his pals, giggling and flirting, so we can easily file reports on your comings and goings."

Carmella and Harmony looked at one another. "We won't do it anymore," said Harmony.

"We promise," Carmella chimed in.

"We'll burn the book."

"To ashes."

"Scram," ordered Chord. "I can't stand the sight of you." Carmella and Harmony backed away and then dashed up the deMichaels' steps.

"Do you believe them?" Sharp asked.

"Not for a New York minute," Chord replied.

Imaginary Enemy

"**W**e're doing a show at school. Want to come?" Sharp asked.

"I'm already going, if it's the one on Friday night. Zander's doing a monologue."

"I forgot about Zander. Jazz is a stagehand and Chord's doing lights. I'm playing a song I wrote."

"Wow. That's impressive. What sort of song?"

"It's a surprise. Wait and see."

Friday evening, Mom, Dad, Carmella, and I piled into a row of seats next to Elliot, Peggy, and Harmony. Imagine my shock when, while waiting for the show to begin, I scanned the program for Sharp's name and saw the title of the song he had written. "Imaginary Enemy."

Sharp's was one of the final performances. When the MC announced his name, he emerged from behind the curtain wearing black dress pants and a white tuxedo shirt. He held a classical guitar. He smiled as the spotlight focused on him. I thought he looked handsome and confident.

Standing before the microphone, he said, "This song is for Gabriel."

"Who's Gabriel?" Mom whispered to Peggy, who shrugged, looking confused. Sharp sat on a wooden stool and began to play an instrumental I knew he'd written just for me. And even though the auditorium was crowded, I felt like he and I were the only two people in the entire world while his fingers danced over the strings.

When I got home that night, I pulled out my blue folder.

> Dear Bubba,
>   Thanks for listening.
>   Your friend,
>   Gabriel

ACKNOWLEDGMENTS

Thanks to my brother-in-law Chief Marc Sackman 702 of the Ferry Pass Fire Department, my family, and my editor, Françoise Bui.